D0916998

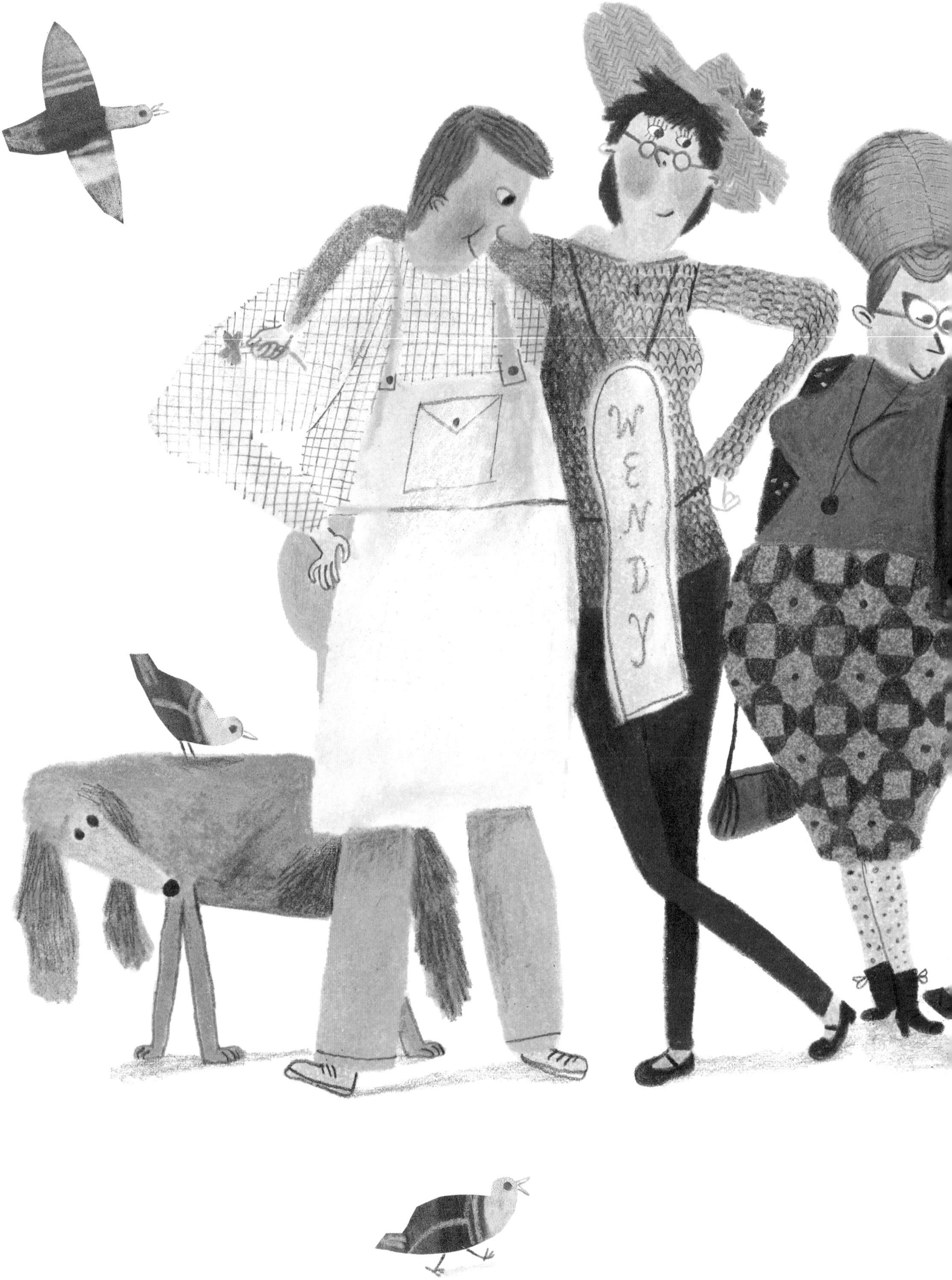
WENDY

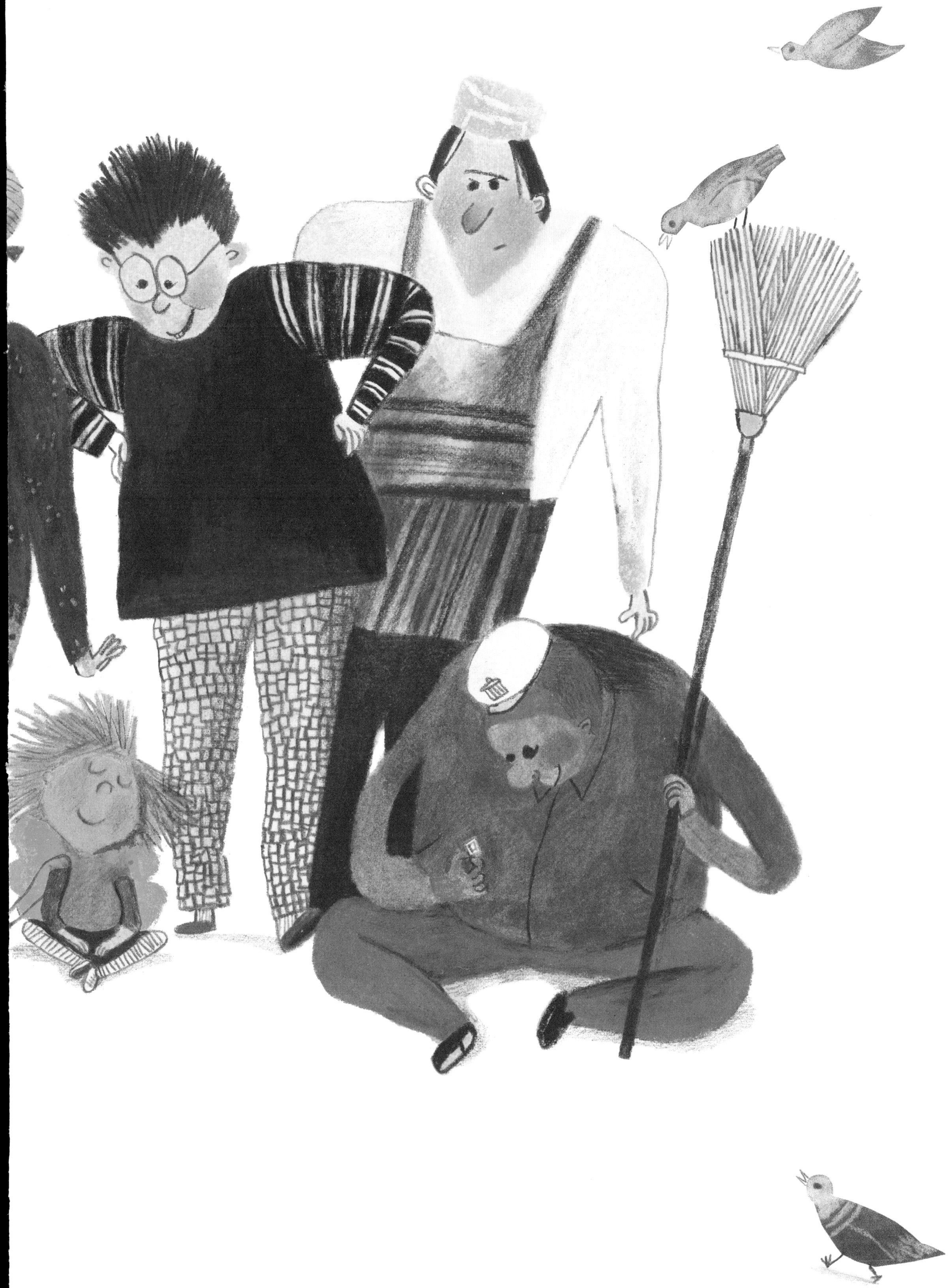

Educ.
JE
ALE

"It's best for young children to live an orderly life. Especially if they order it themselves."

–Fifi Brindacier

My thanks to Paola, Béatrice, Olivier, Emmanuel, William and Alix. — B. A.

enchantedlionbooks.com

First American edition published in 2015 by Enchanted Lion Books,
351 Van Brunt Street, Brooklyn, NY 11231
Translated from the French by Claudia Zoe Bedrick
Copyright © 2015 by Enchanted Lion for the English-language translation
Originally published in France in 2014 as *Le merveilleux Dodu-Velu-Petit*
Copyright © 2014 by Albin Michel Jeunesse
All rights reserved under International and Pan-American Copyright Conventions
A CIP record is on file with the Library of Congress
ISBN 978-1-59270-180-3

Second Printing 2016
Printed in China by Toppan Leefung

10 9 8 7 6 5 4 3 2

BEATRICE ALEMAGNA

THE WONDERFUL
Fluffy Little Squishy

ENCHANTED LION BOOKS
NEW YORK

My name is Edith, but my friends call me Eddie. I'm five-and-a-half years old.

My dad speaks five languages,
my mom sings like a bird,
my sister is an ice-skating queen,
but me—I don't know how to do anything.

Nothing at all. That's what I think, anyway.

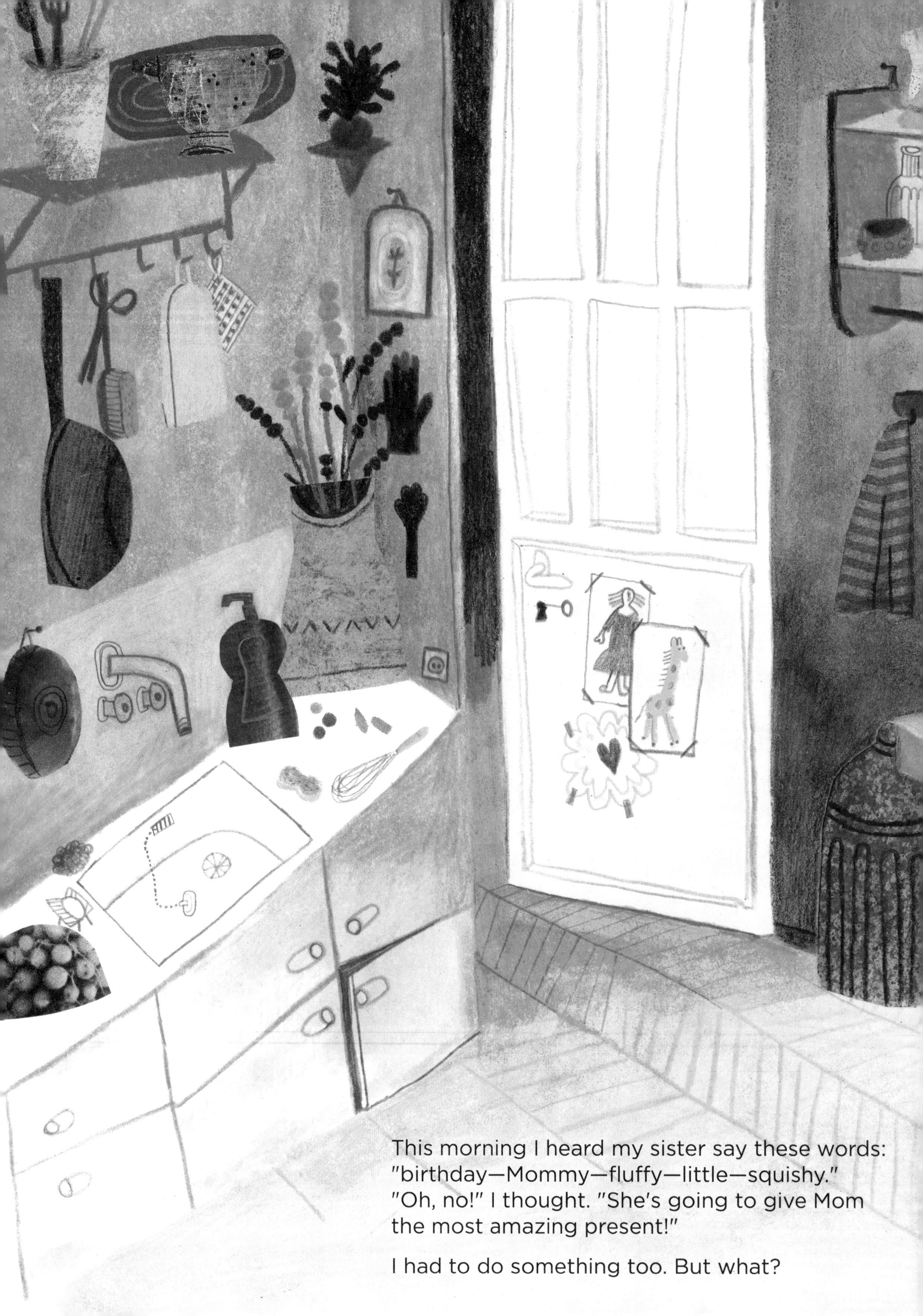

This morning I heard my sister say these words:
"birthday—Mommy—fluffy—little—squishy."
"Oh, no!" I thought. "She's going to give Mom the most amazing present!"

I had to do something too. But what?

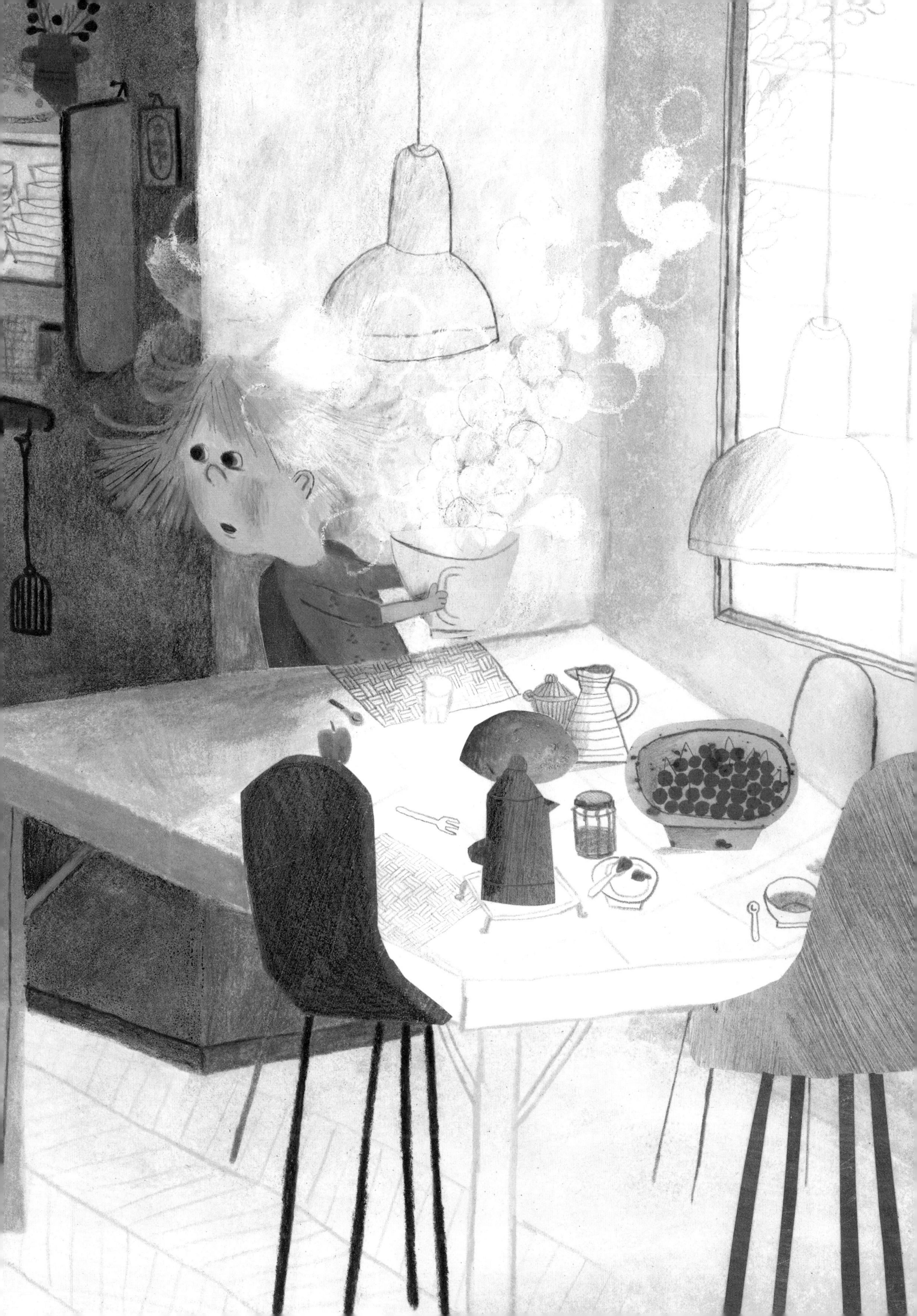

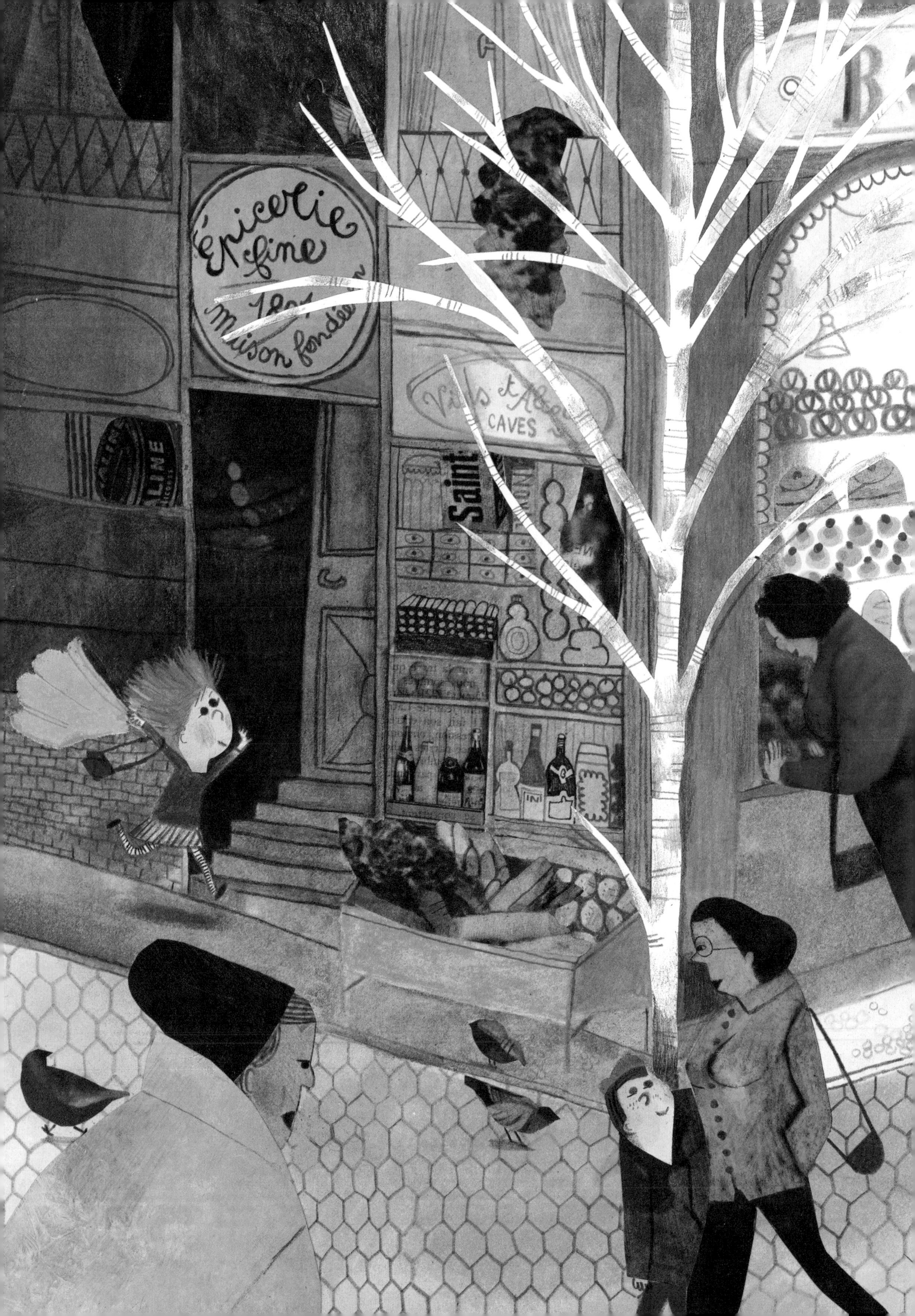
Épicerie fine
Maison fondée
CAVES
Saint

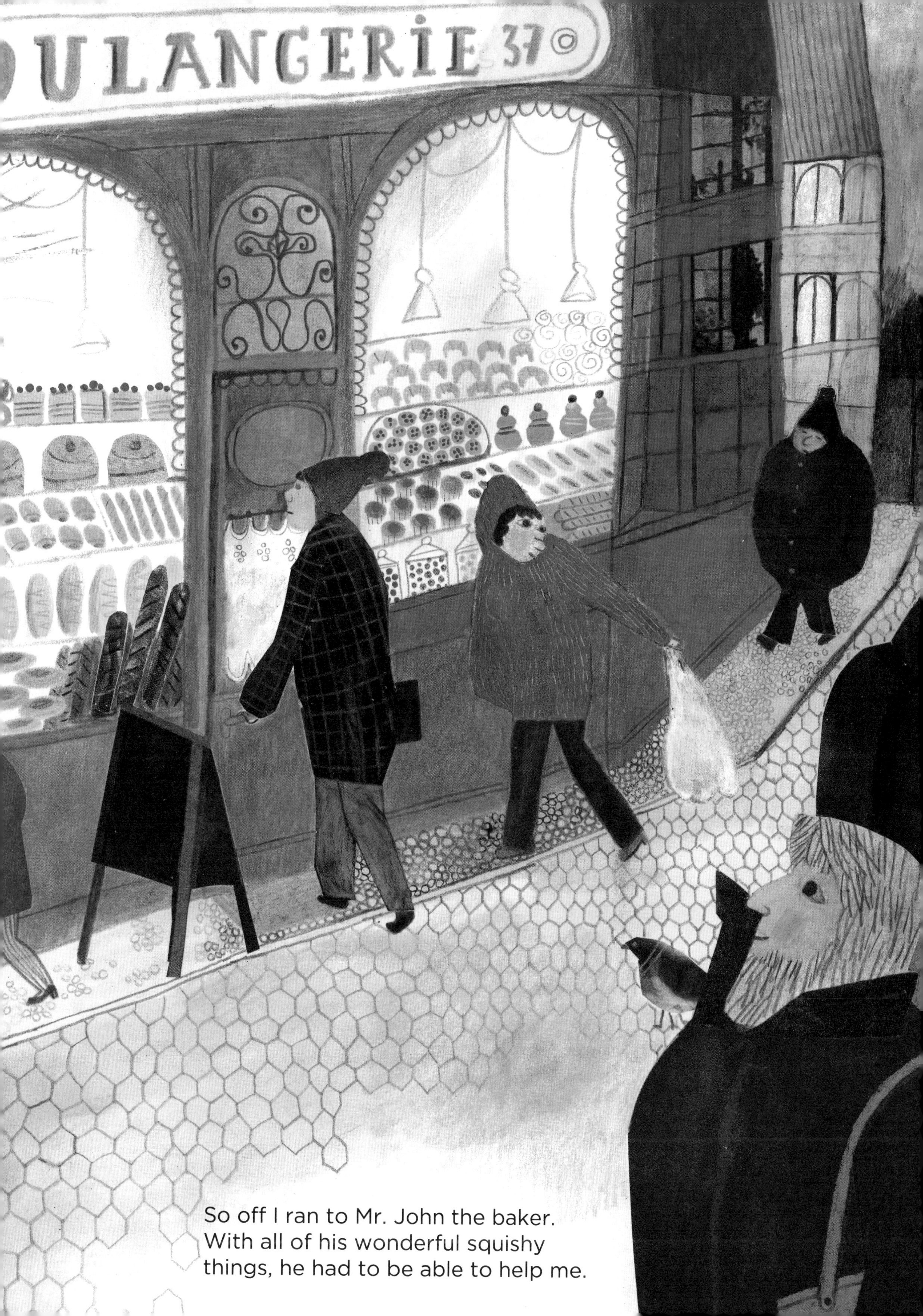
ULANGERIE 37

So off I ran to Mr. John the baker.
With all of his wonderful squishy
things, he had to be able to help me.

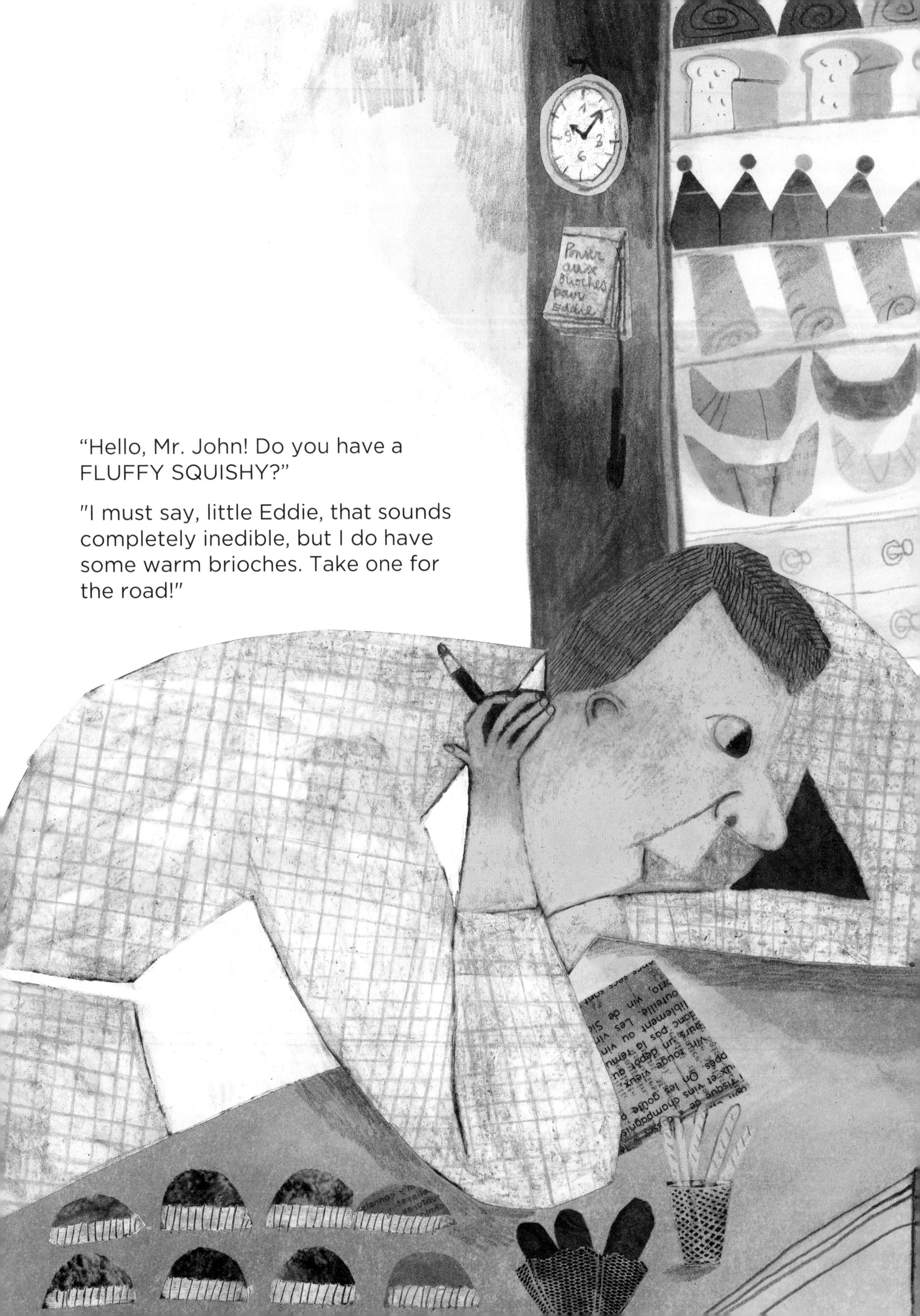

"Hello, Mr. John! Do you have a FLUFFY SQUISHY?"

"I must say, little Eddie, that sounds completely inedible, but I do have some warm brioches. Take one for the road!"

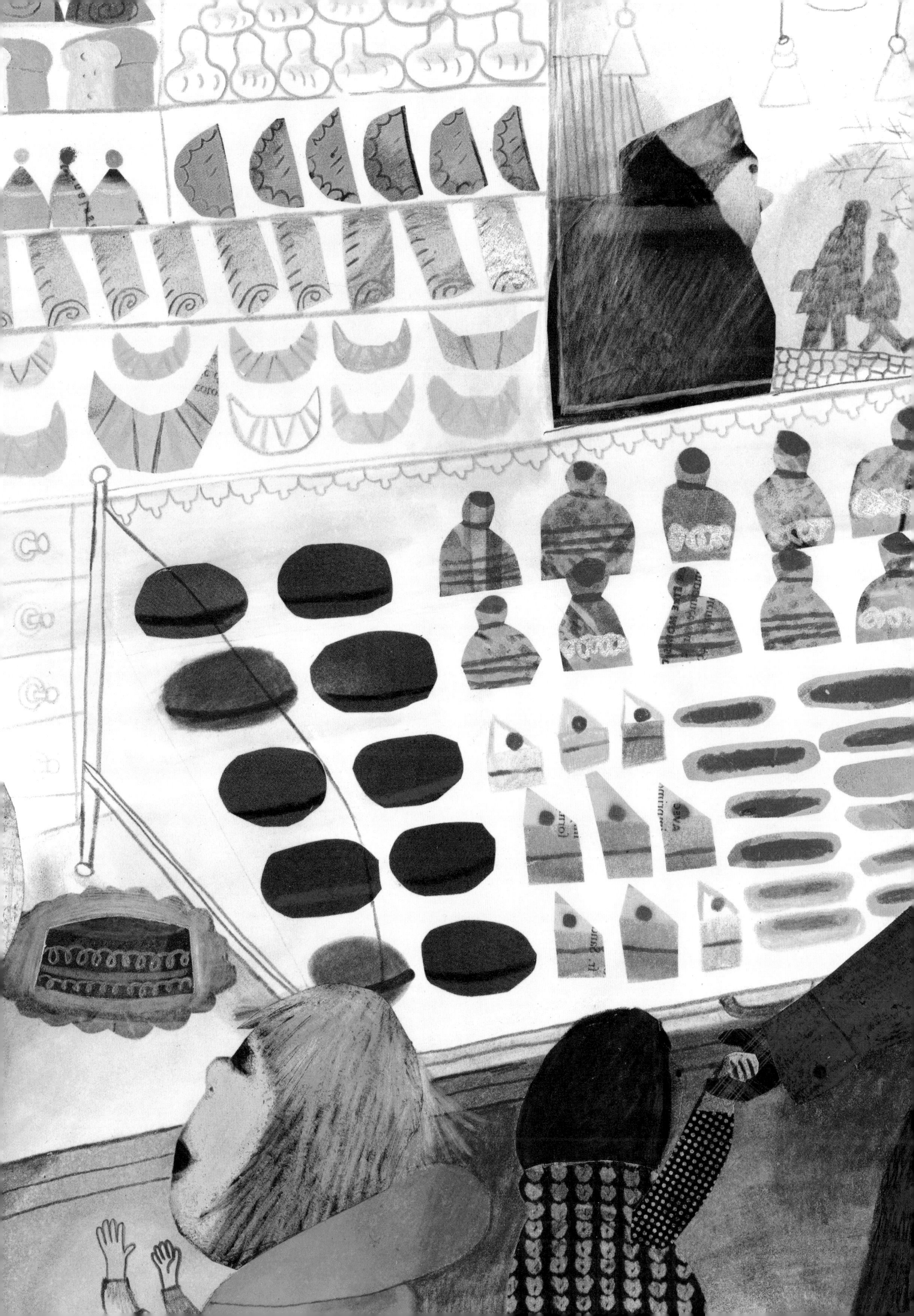

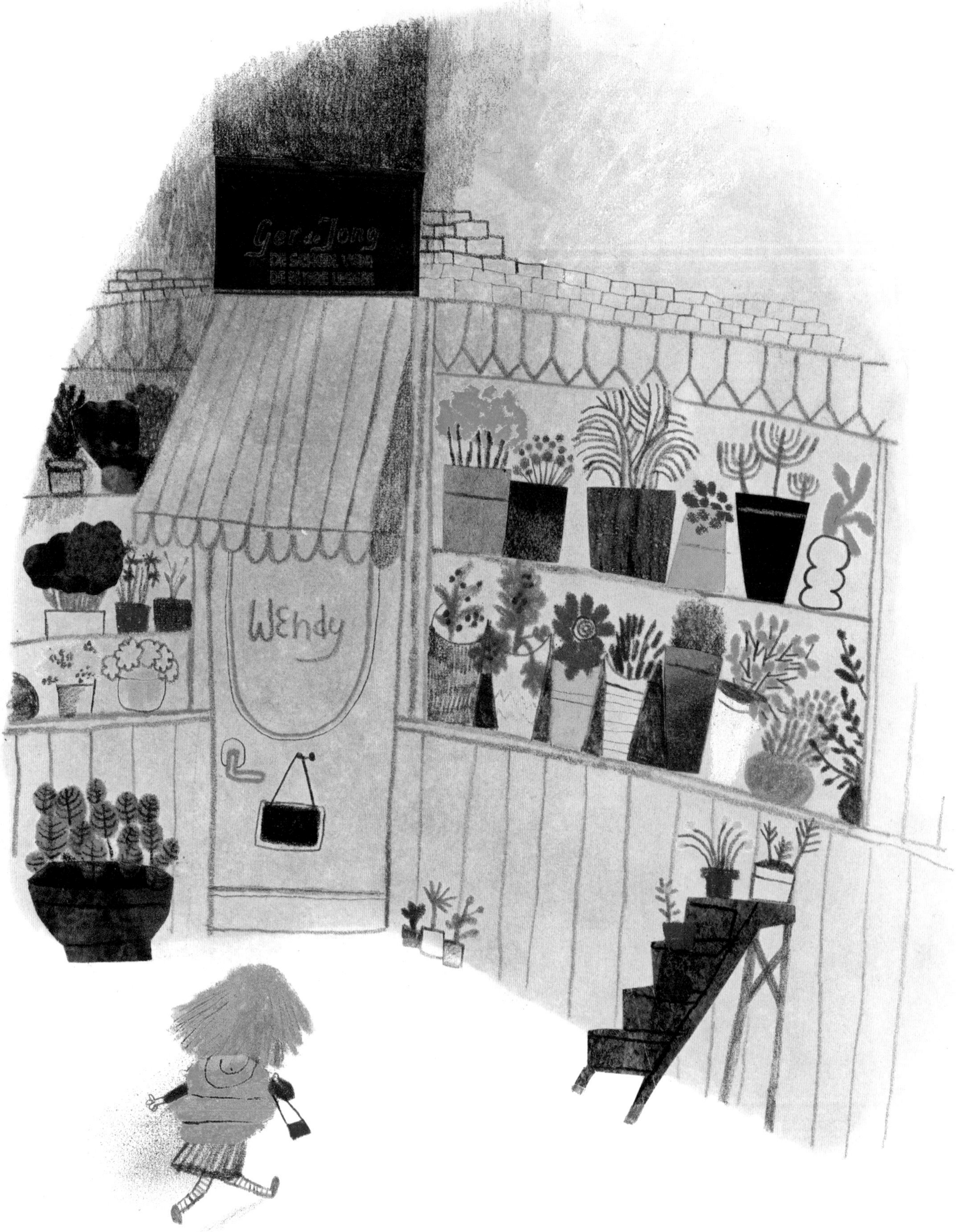
Ger de Jong
Wendy

I tucked the brioche into my bag and set off to see
Wendy, the prettiest florist in the whole neighborhood.

"A TUFTY FLUFFY? That must be a fuzzy plant," Wendy decided. "Take this clover. It will bring you good luck."

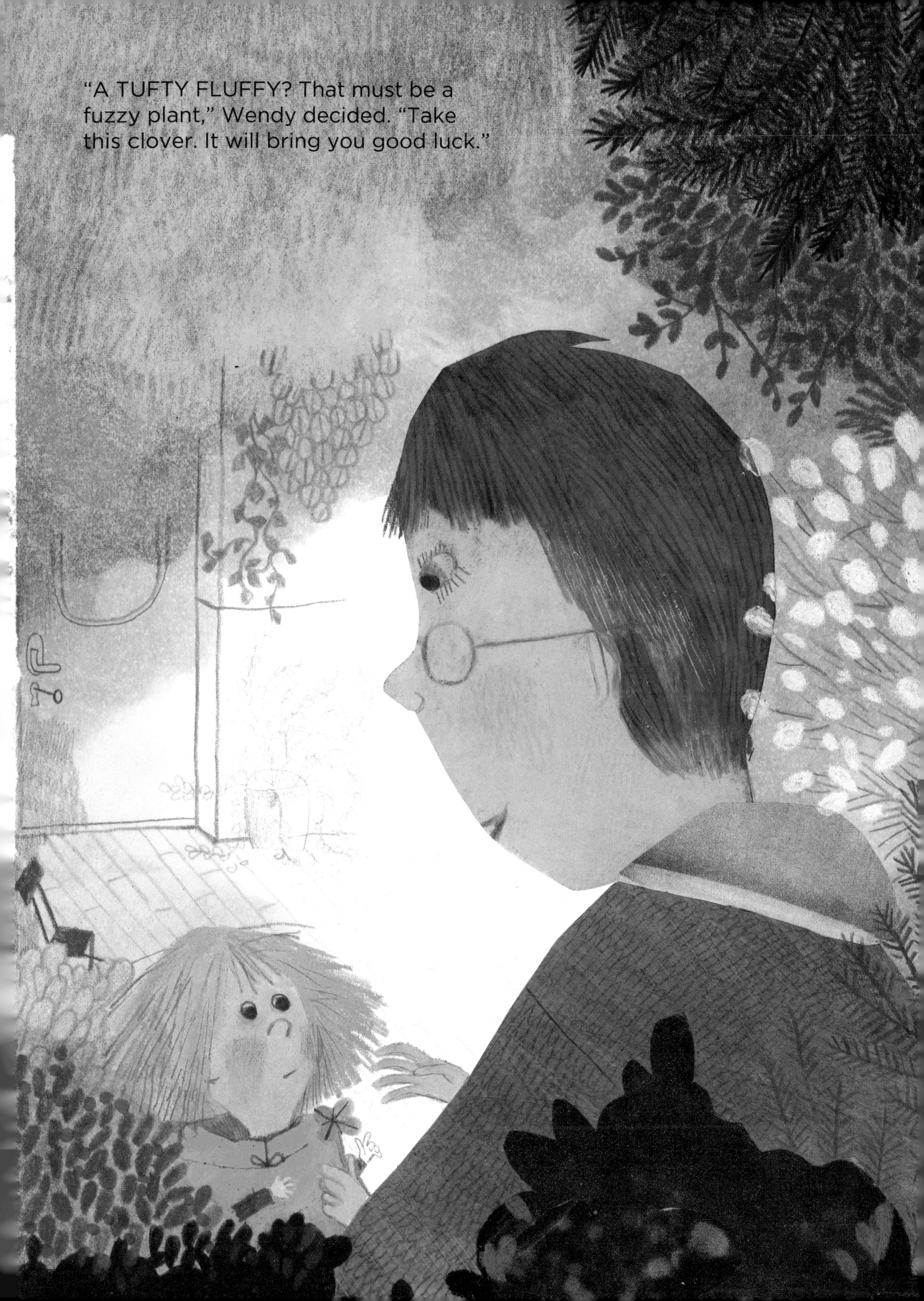

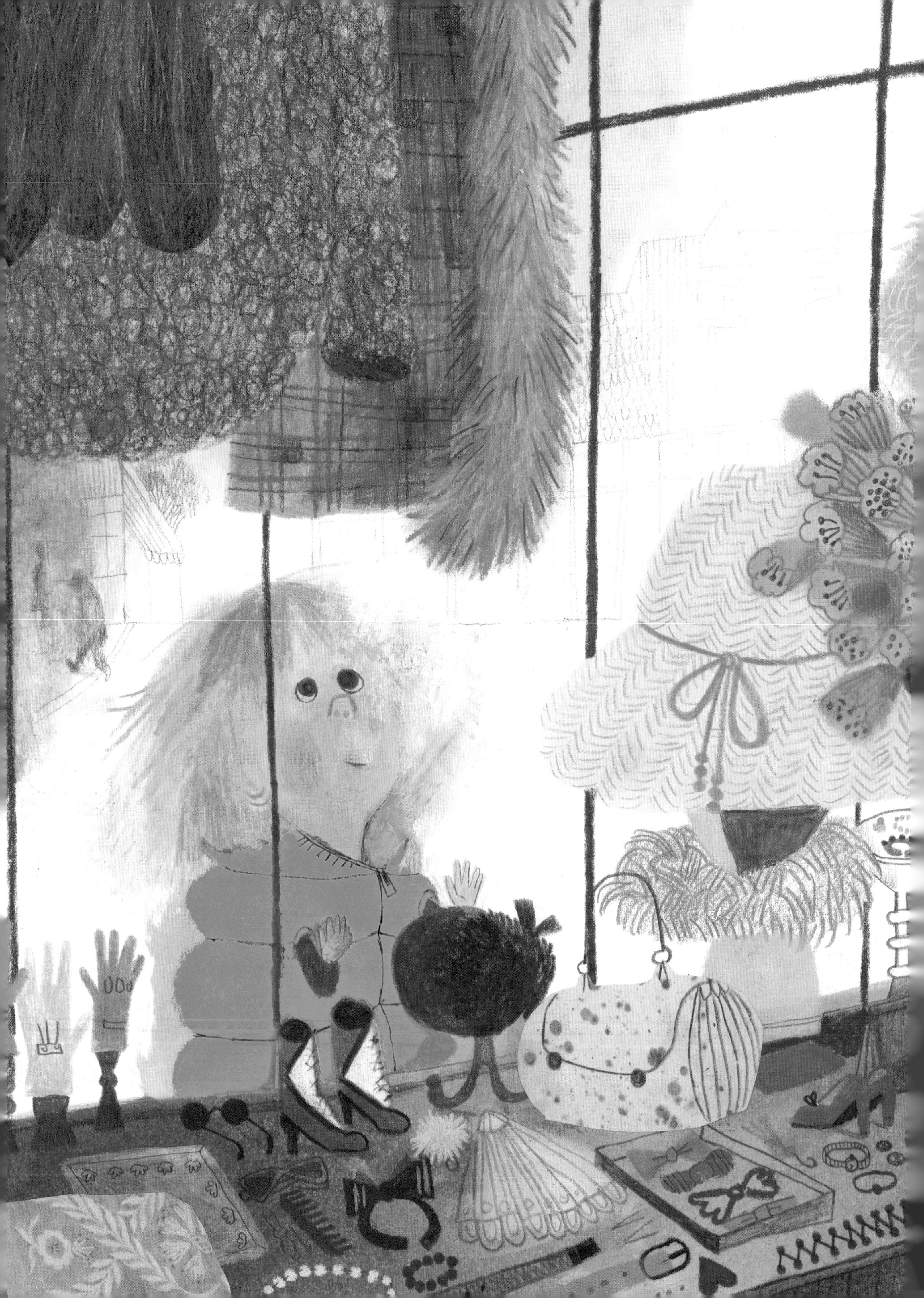

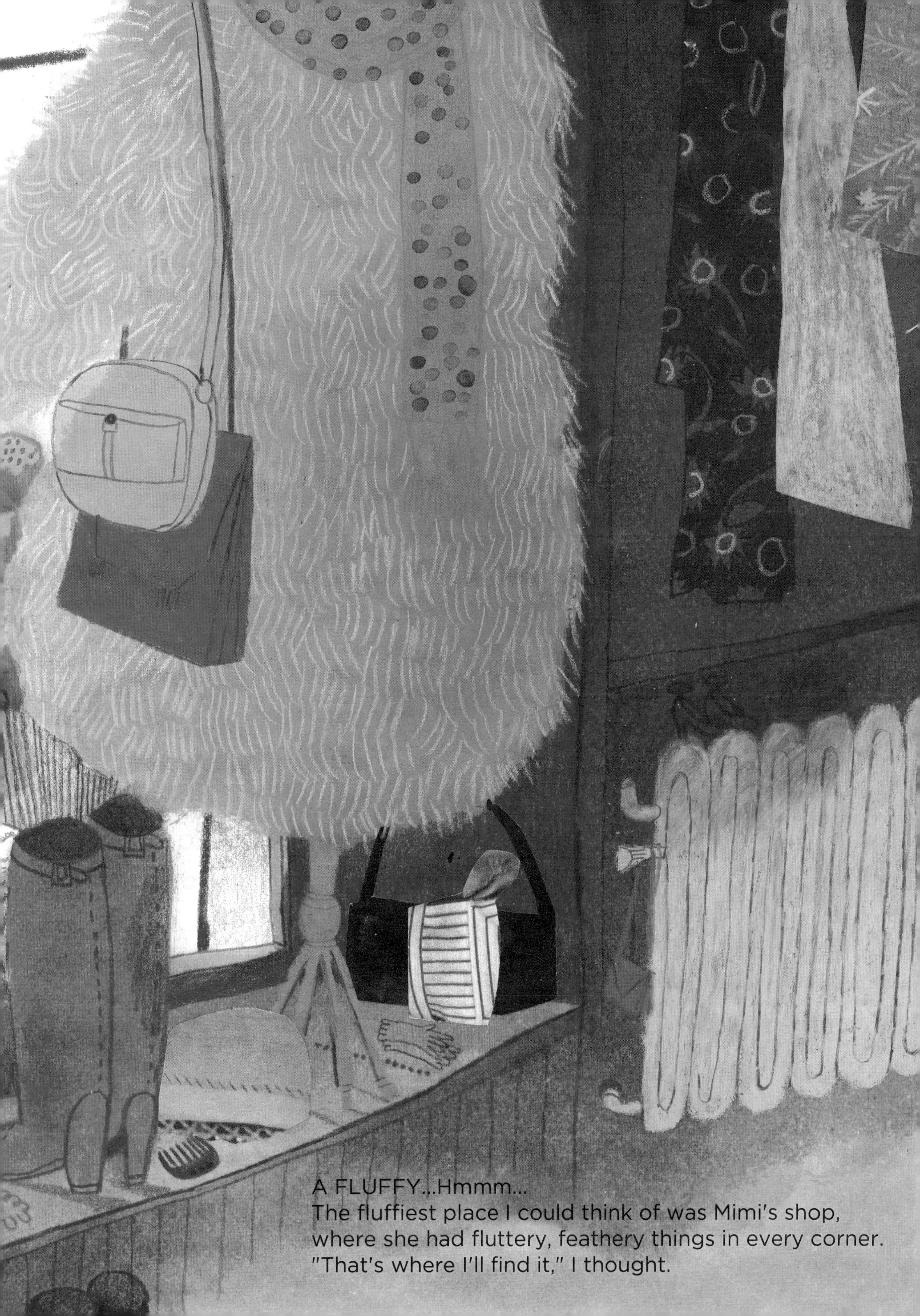

A FLUFFY...Hmmm...
The fluffiest place I could think of was Mimi's shop, where she had fluttery, feathery things in every corner. "That's where I'll find it," I thought.

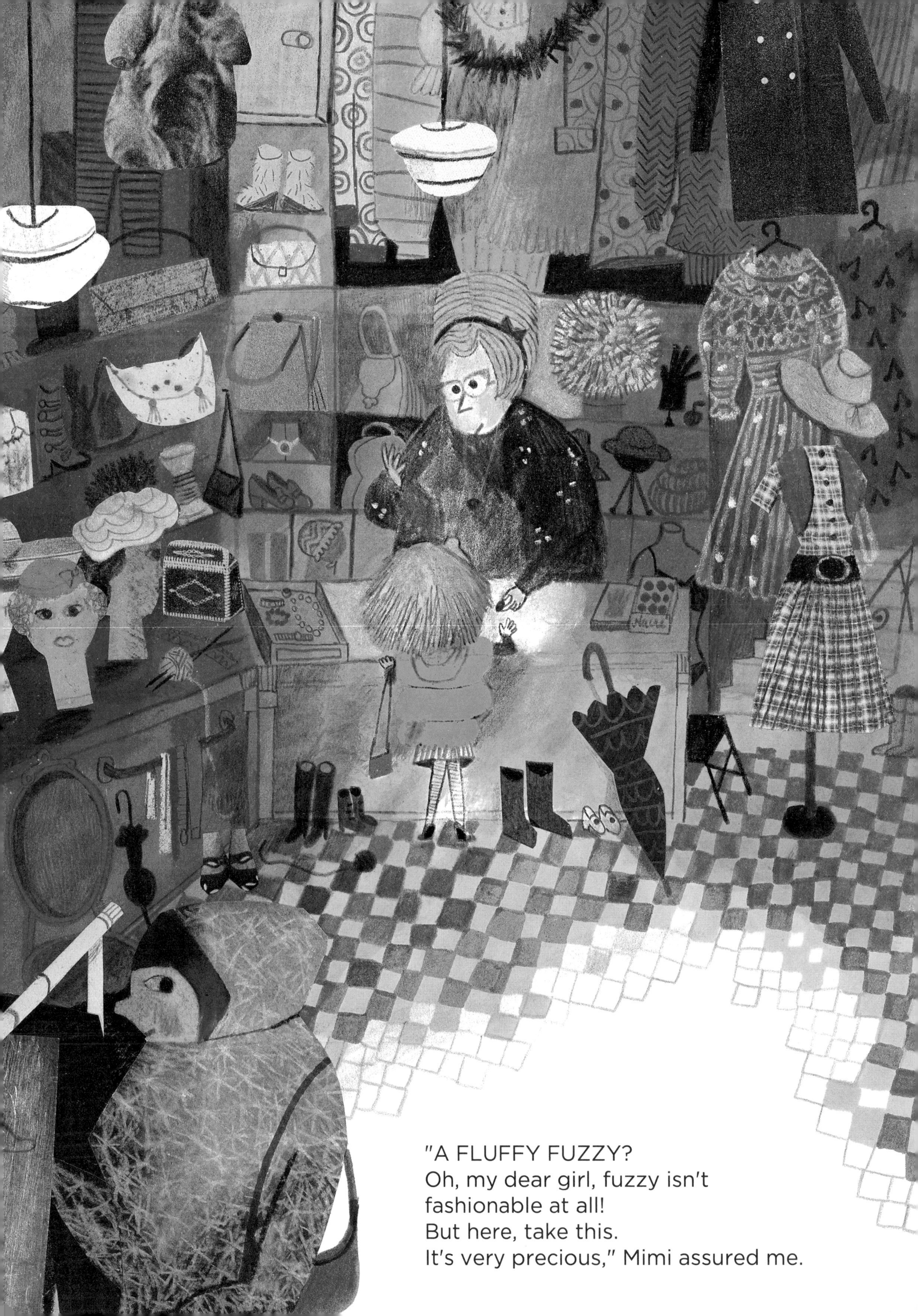

"A FLUFFY FUZZY?
Oh, my dear girl, fuzzy isn't
fashionable at all!
But here, take this.
It's very precious," Mimi assured me.

A mother-of-pearl button? Finally, I was making progress! There was just one more thing for me to do. I had to go see the most fashionable person in the whole wide world.

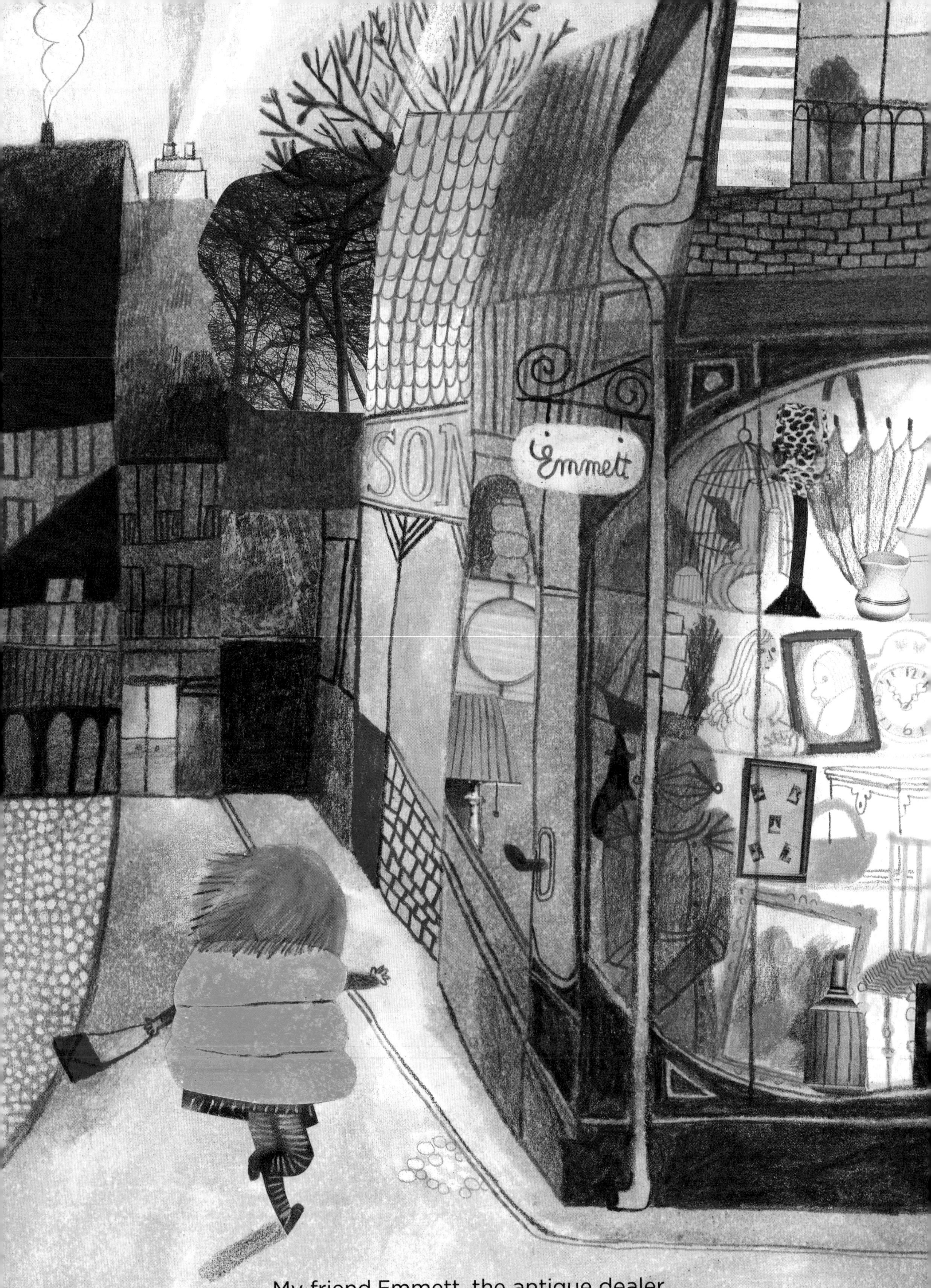
SON
Emmett

My friend Emmett, the antique dealer.

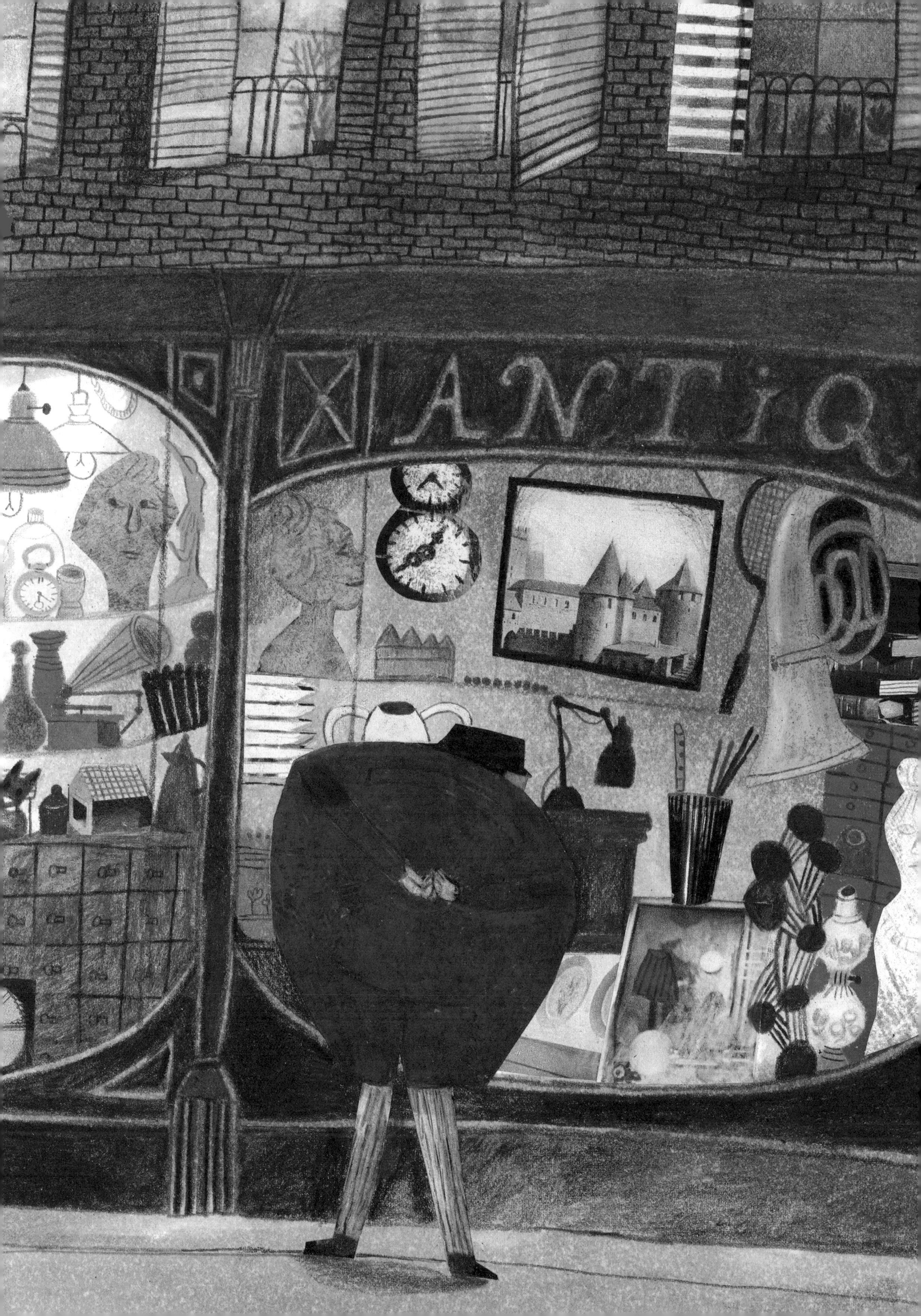
ANTIQ

"A PLUMP WHATSIT?" asked Emmett.
"Hmmm...I don't have anything quite like that, Eddie.
But here is a real treasure for your mother: a stamp
from the British Navy. EX-TRE-ME-LY RARE!
I'm sure she'll love it."

An old stamp?
Maybe things weren't
going so well, after all...

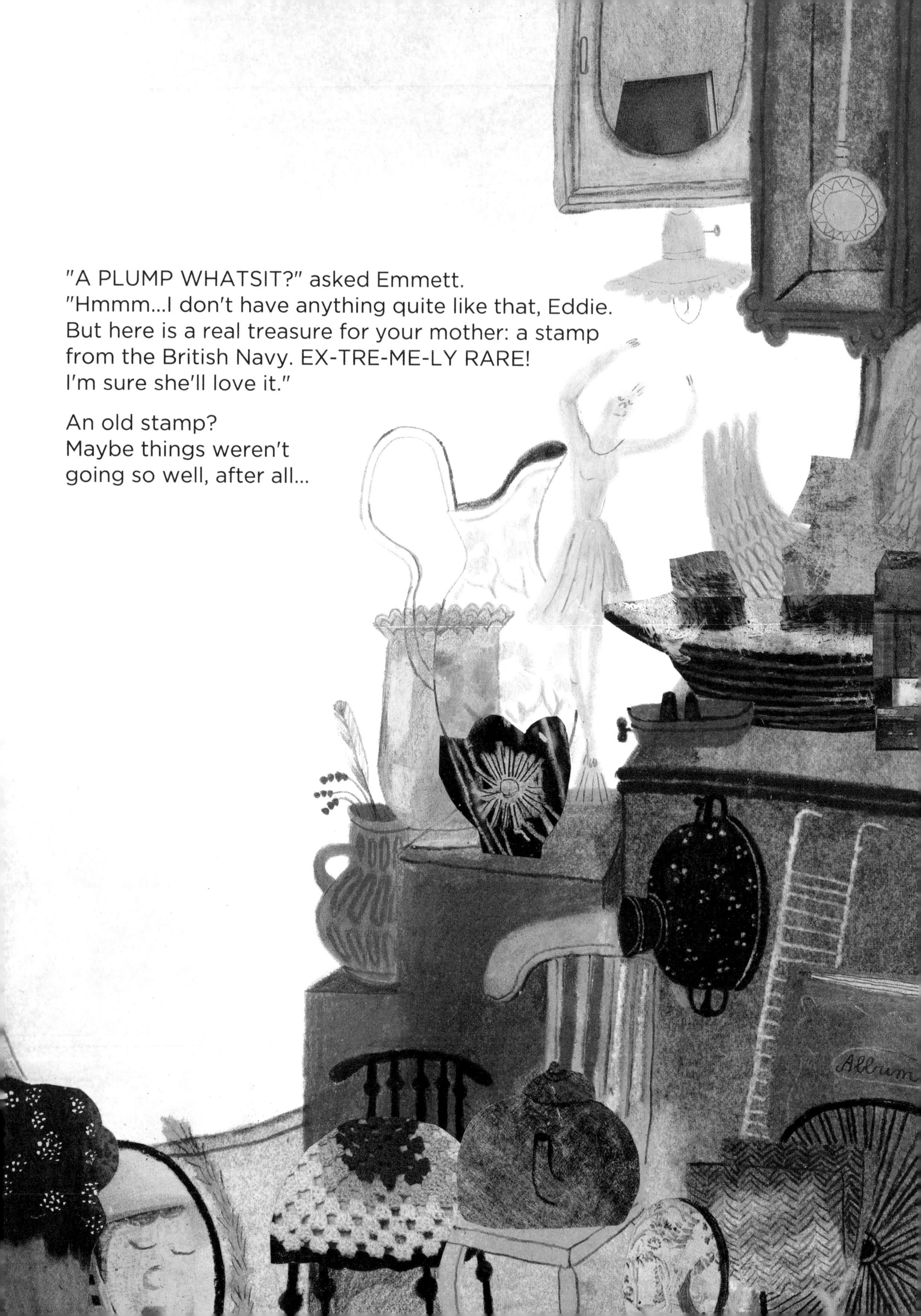
Album

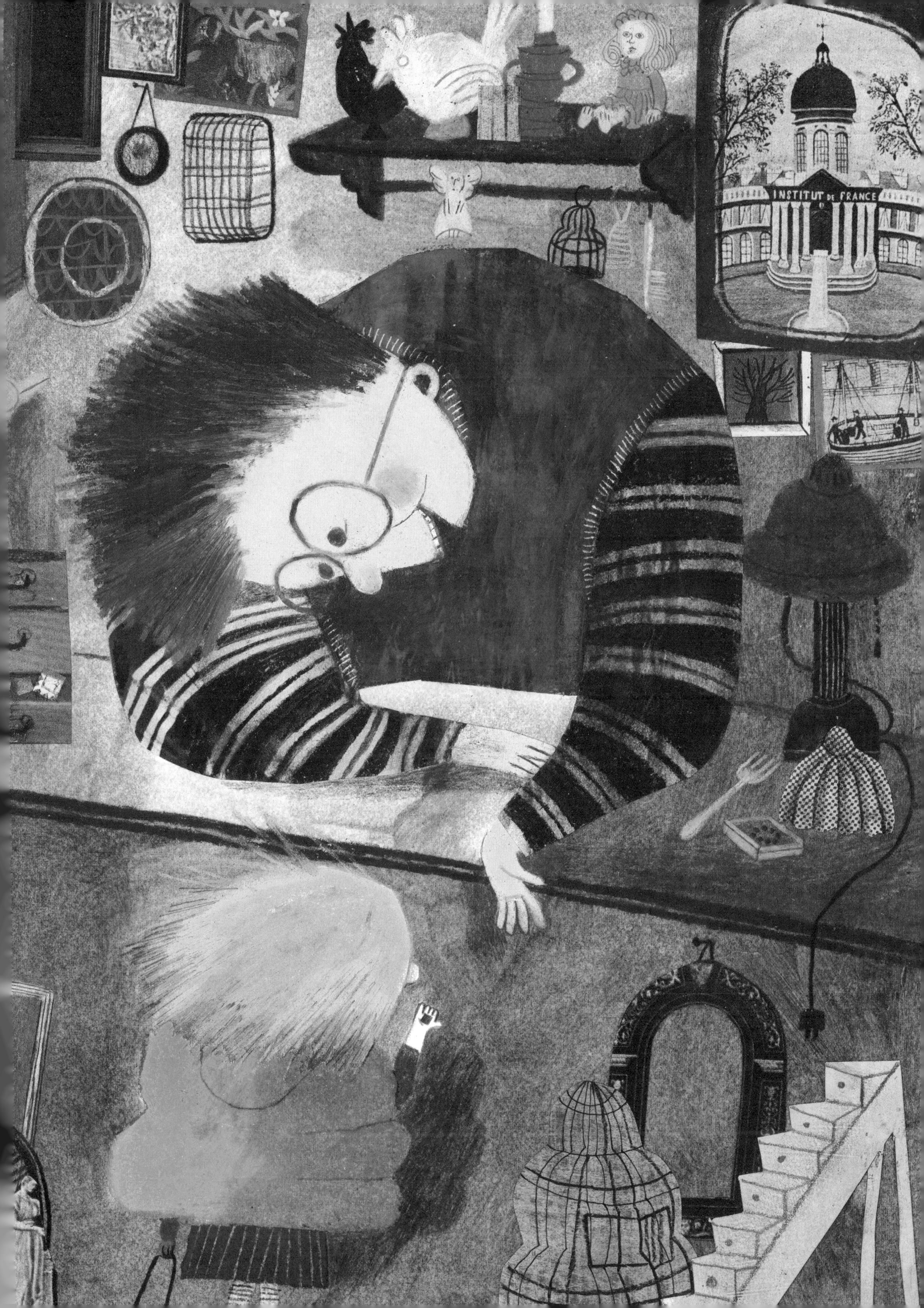
INSTITUT DE FRANCE

I went to every shop in the neighborhood, but nobody knew anything. In the center of town was Theo's butcher shop.

The big grump was my last hope.

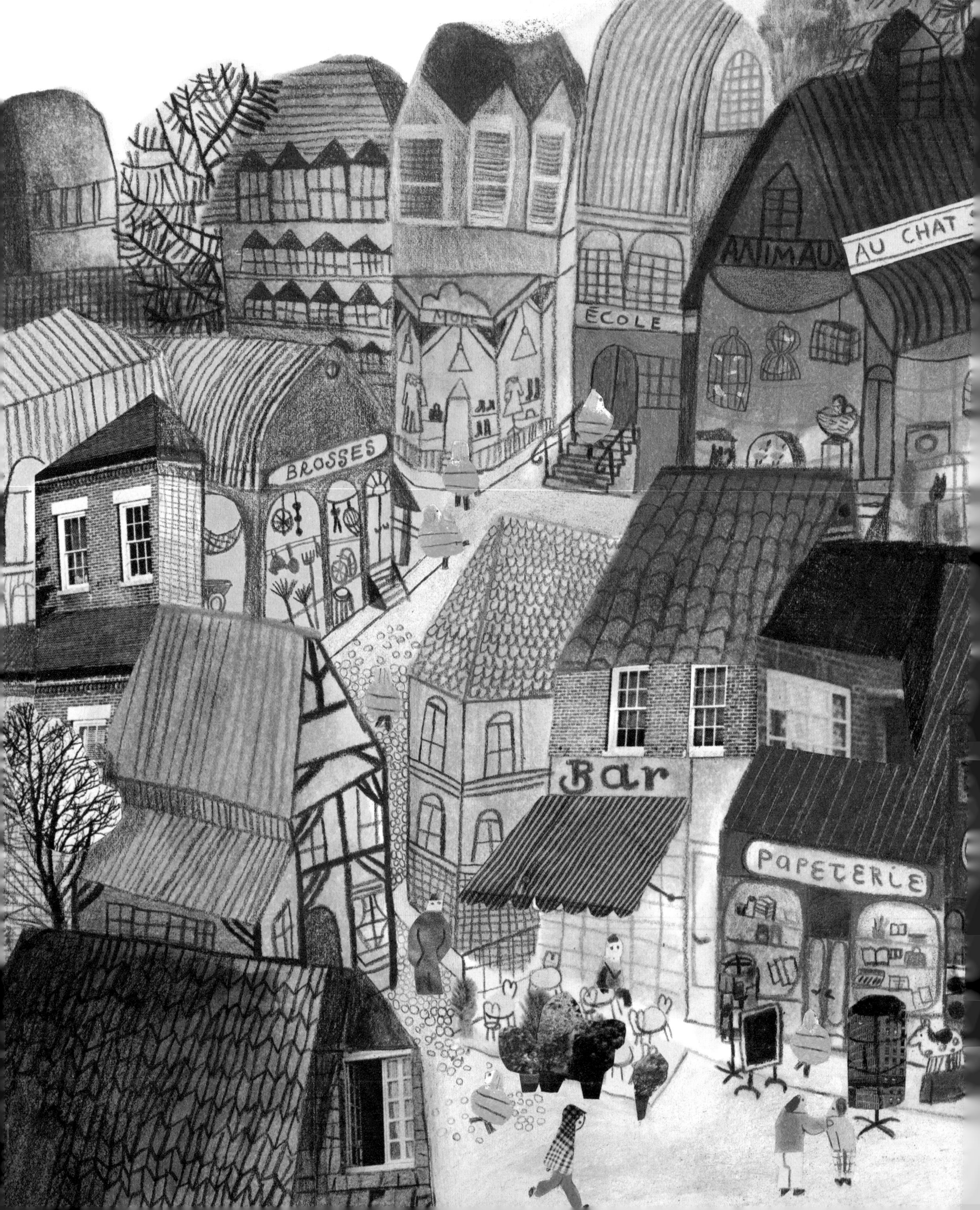
AU CHAT
ÉCOLE
BROSSES
Bar
PAPETERIE

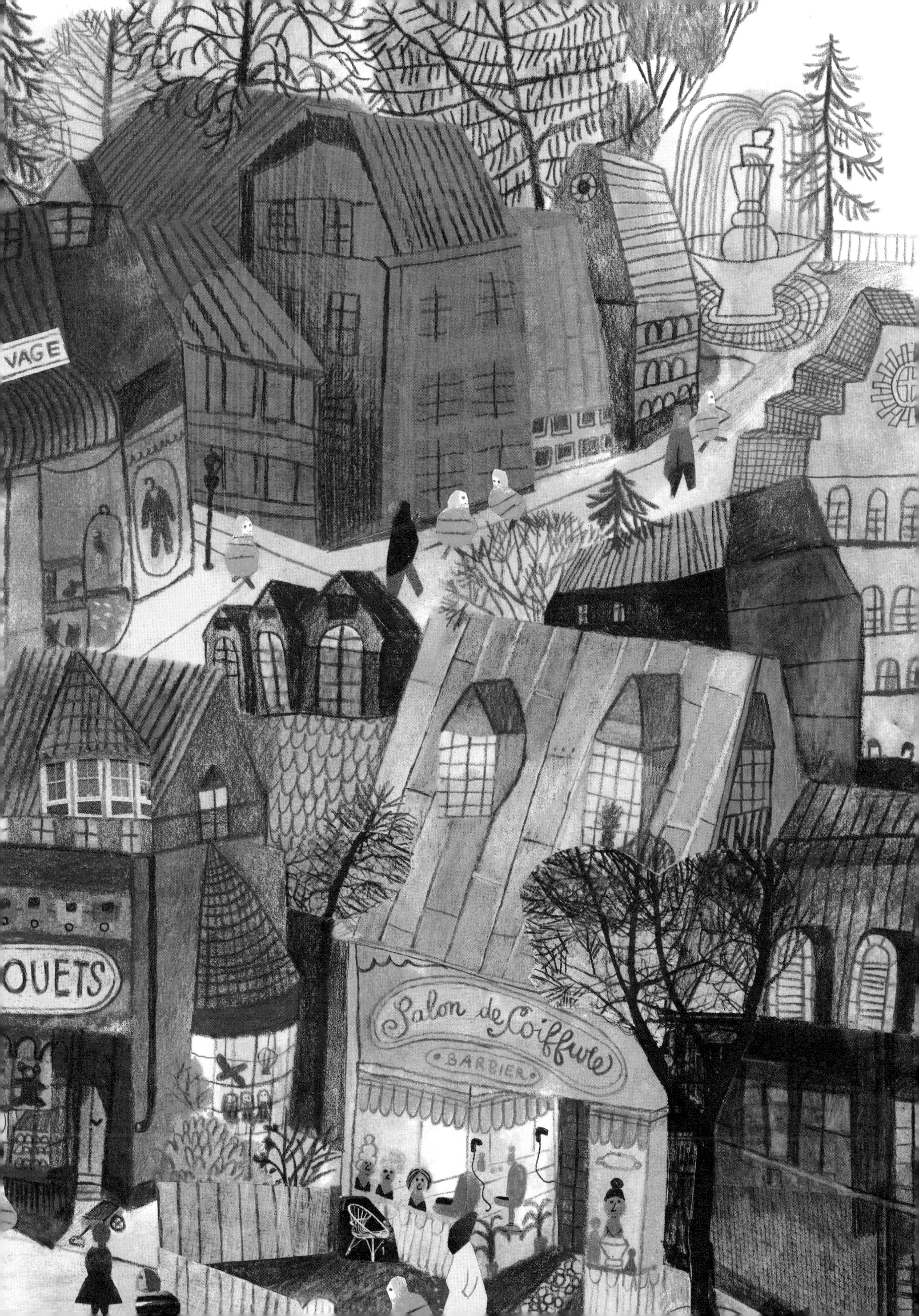
VAGE
OUETS
Salon de Coiffure
BARBIER

"A what? A SILLY SQUISHY?" yelled Theo, pointing his big knife right at my nose. "I don't have time for such foolishness! Go on, get out of here, Eddie!"

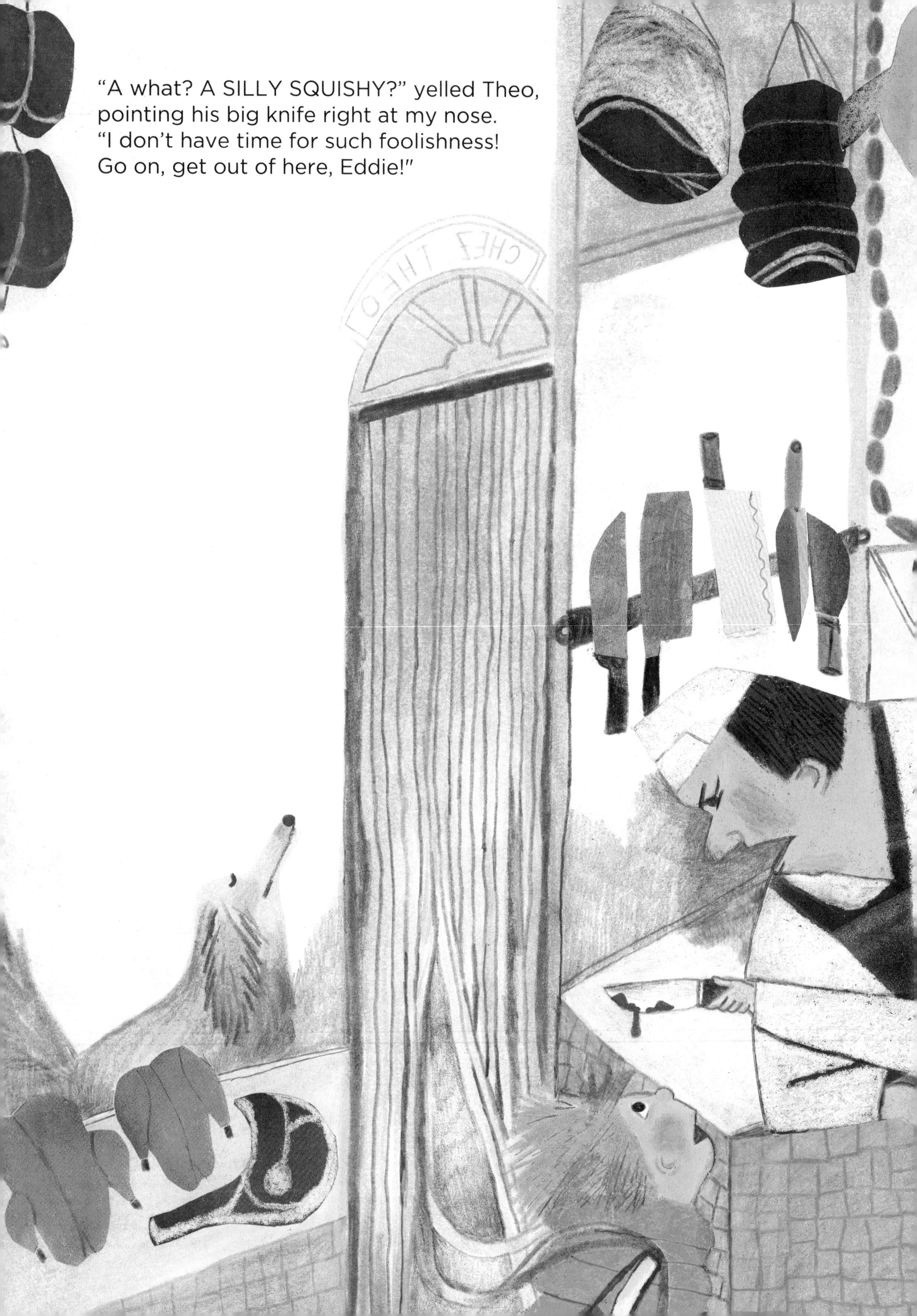
CHEZ THEO

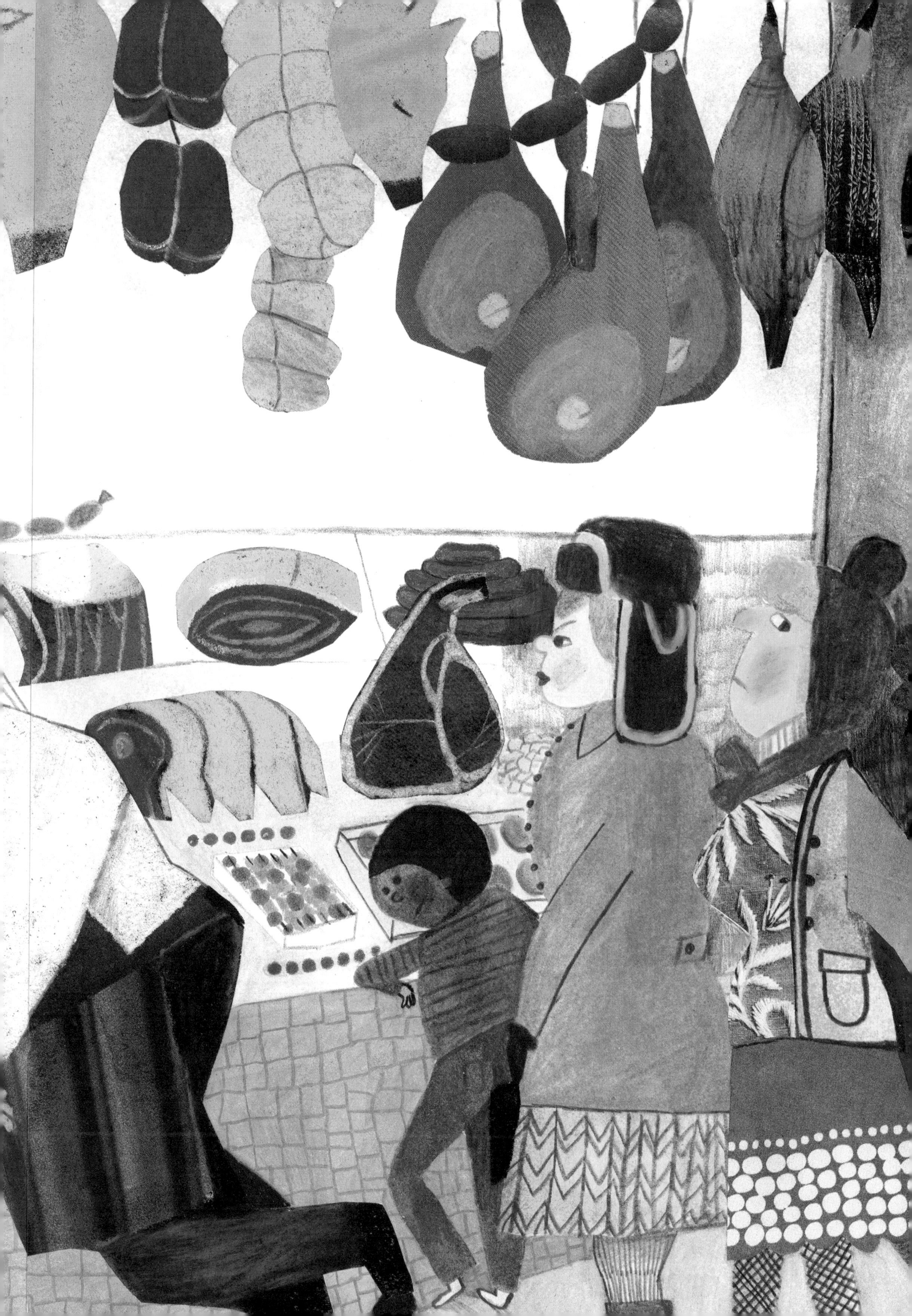

AAAHHHH!
I was so scared that I ran out of there as fast as a jack rabbit.

Darn it all!
And now it was snowing.
I felt so tired and discouraged that I looked for a place to rest.

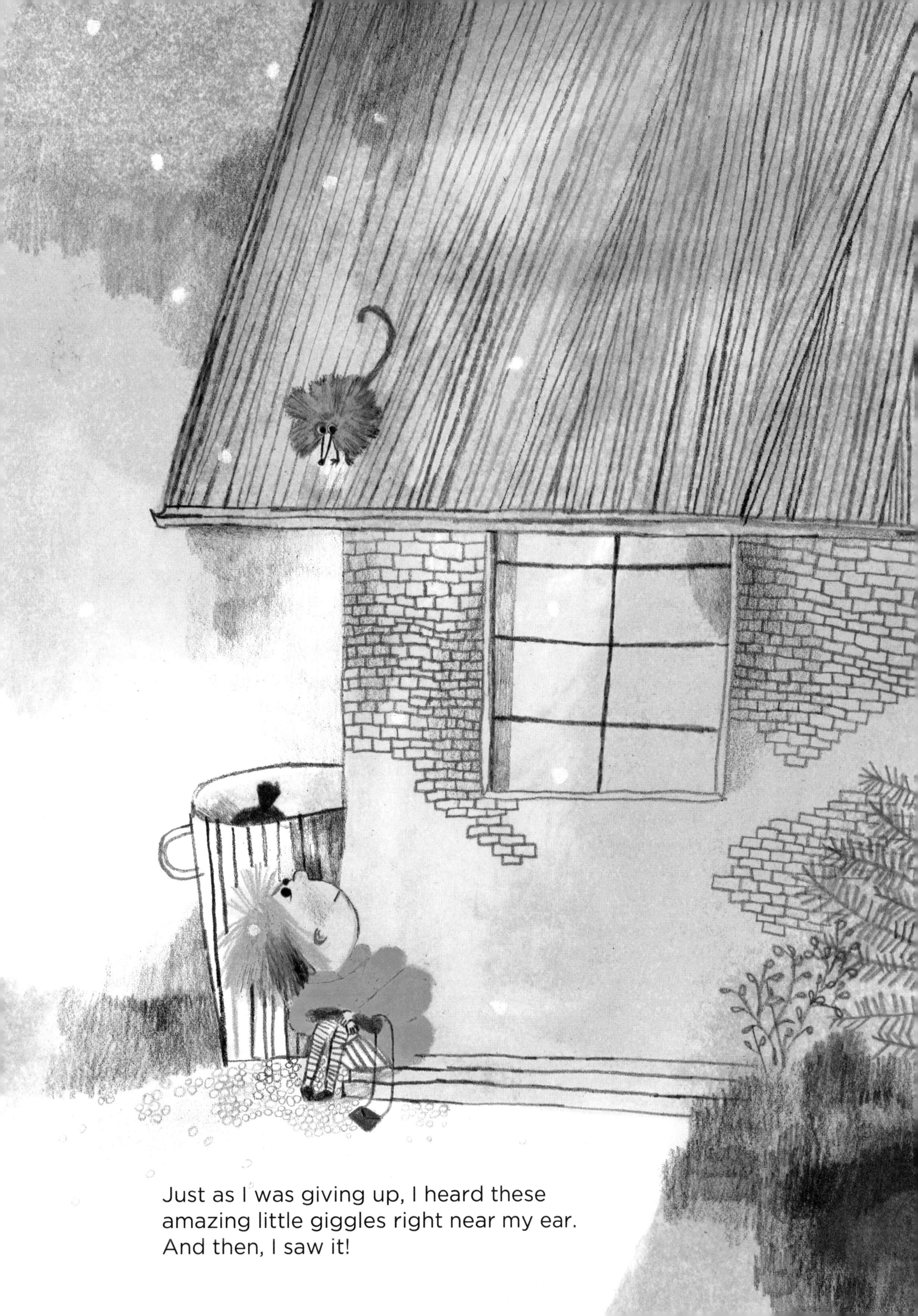

Just as I was giving up, I heard these amazing little giggles right near my ear. And then, I saw it!

It was an adorable little creature!
Fluffy, inedible, not stylish, and rare.
A true FLUFFY LITTLE SQUISHY, at last!
My present with a thousand uses!

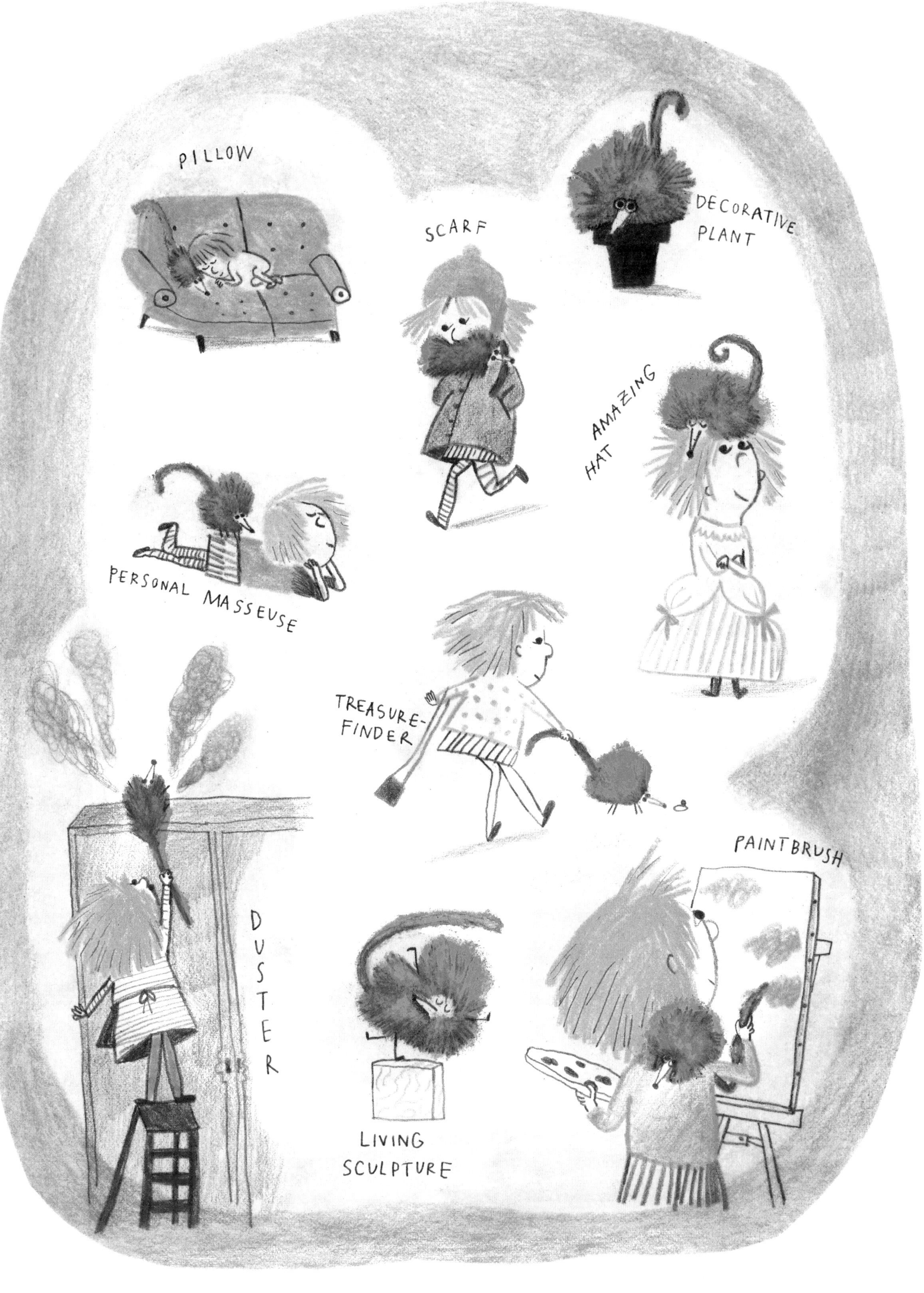
PILLOW
SCARF
DECORATIVE PLANT
AMAZING HAT
PERSONAL MASSEUSE
TREASURE-FINDER
DUSTER
PAINTBRUSH
LIVING SCULPTURE

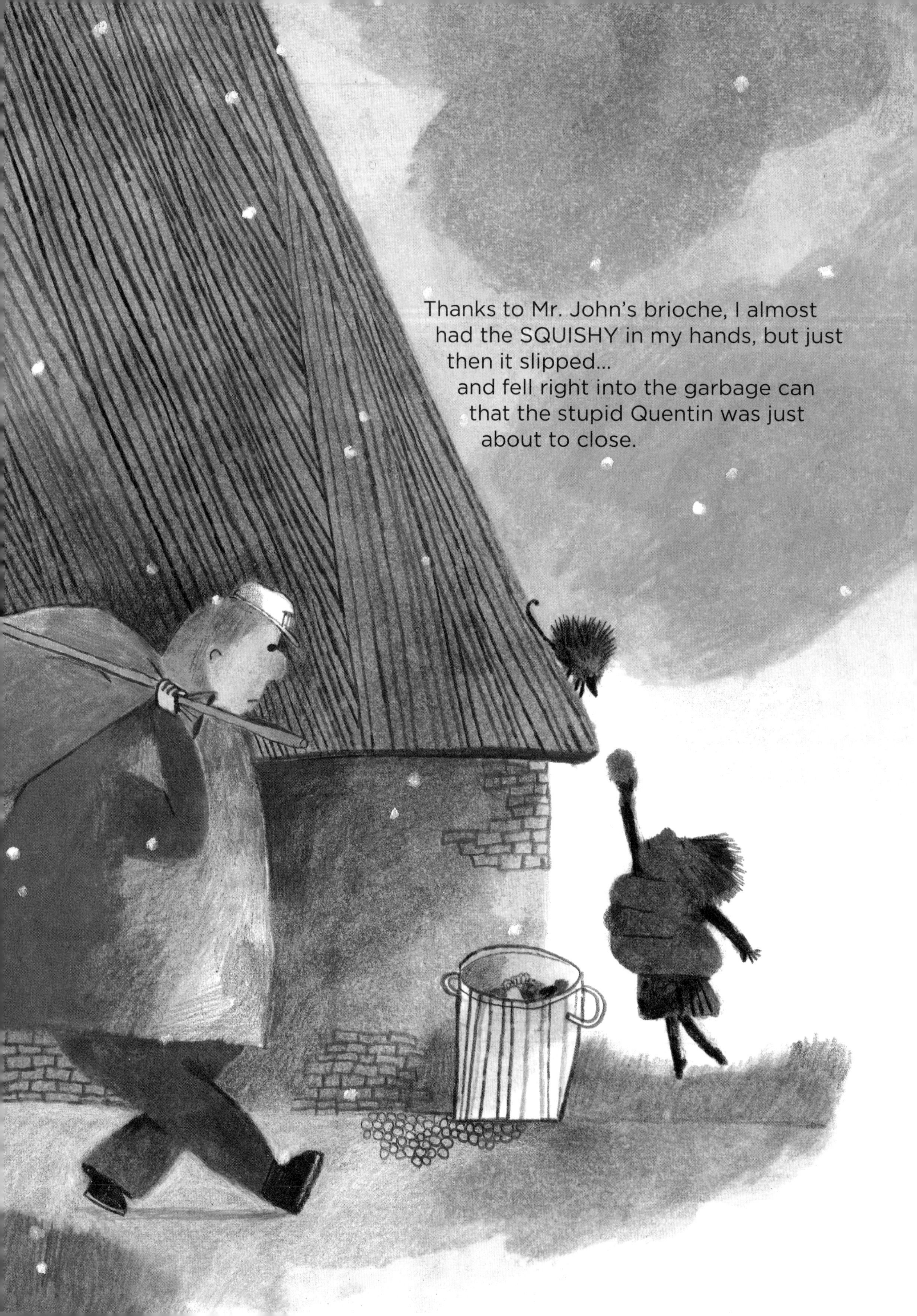

Thanks to Mr. John's brioche, I almost had the SQUISHY in my hands, but just then it slipped...
and fell right into the garbage can that the stupid Quentin was just about to close.

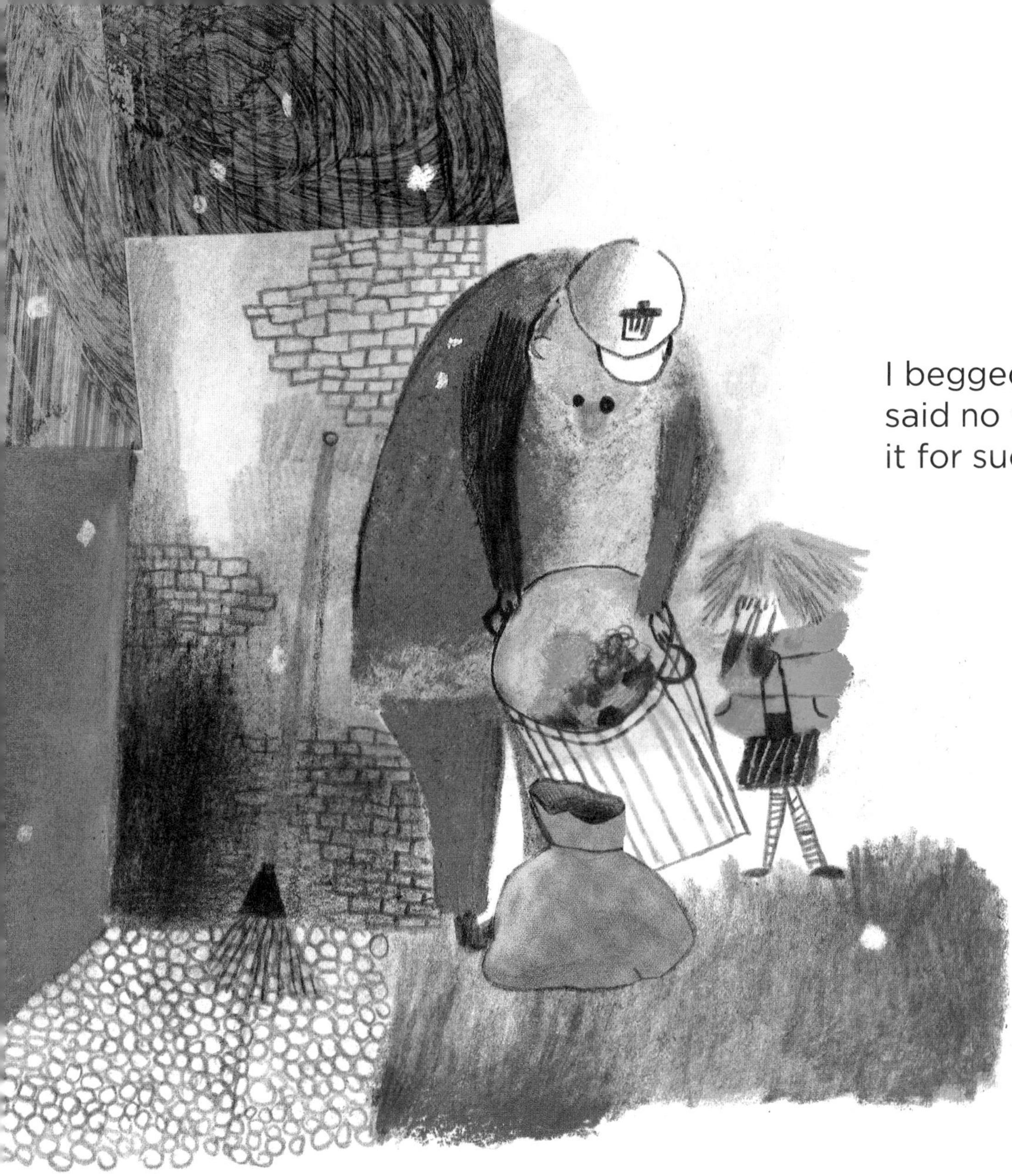

I begged him to stop, but he said no way would he open it for such a dirty old rag.

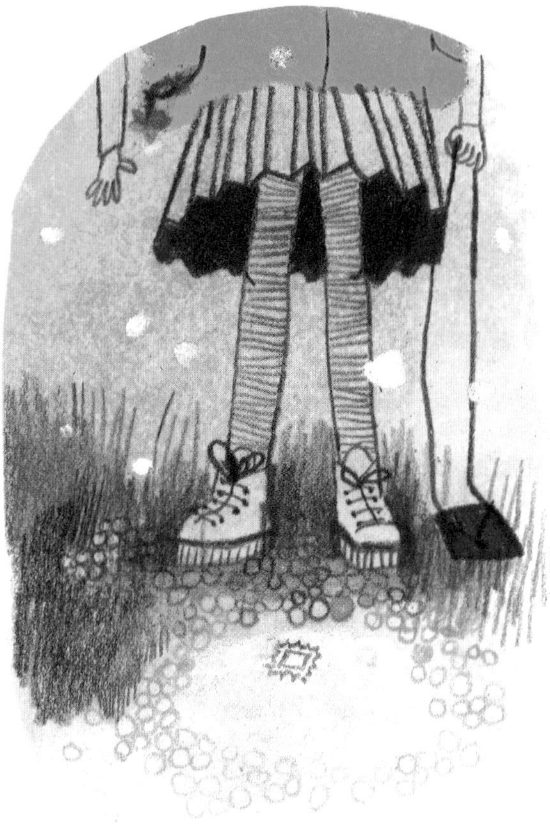

Such bad luck!
I dug in my pocket for Wendy's clover
and the old stamp fell out onto the ground.
Immediately, Quentin swung around.

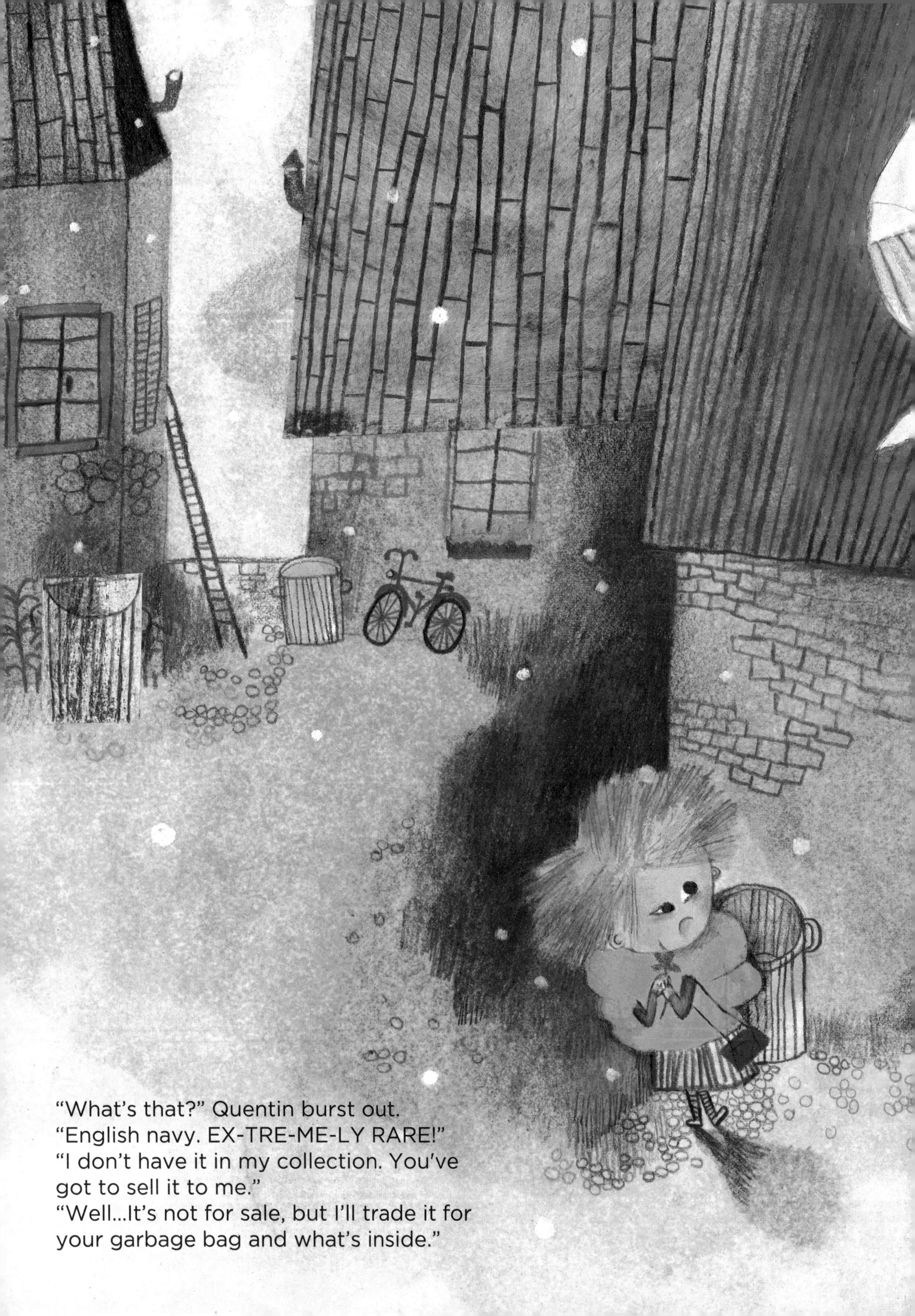

"What's that?" Quentin burst out.
"English navy. EX-TRE-ME-LY RARE!"
"I don't have it in my collection. You've got to sell it to me."
"Well...It's not for sale, but I'll trade it for your garbage bag and what's inside."

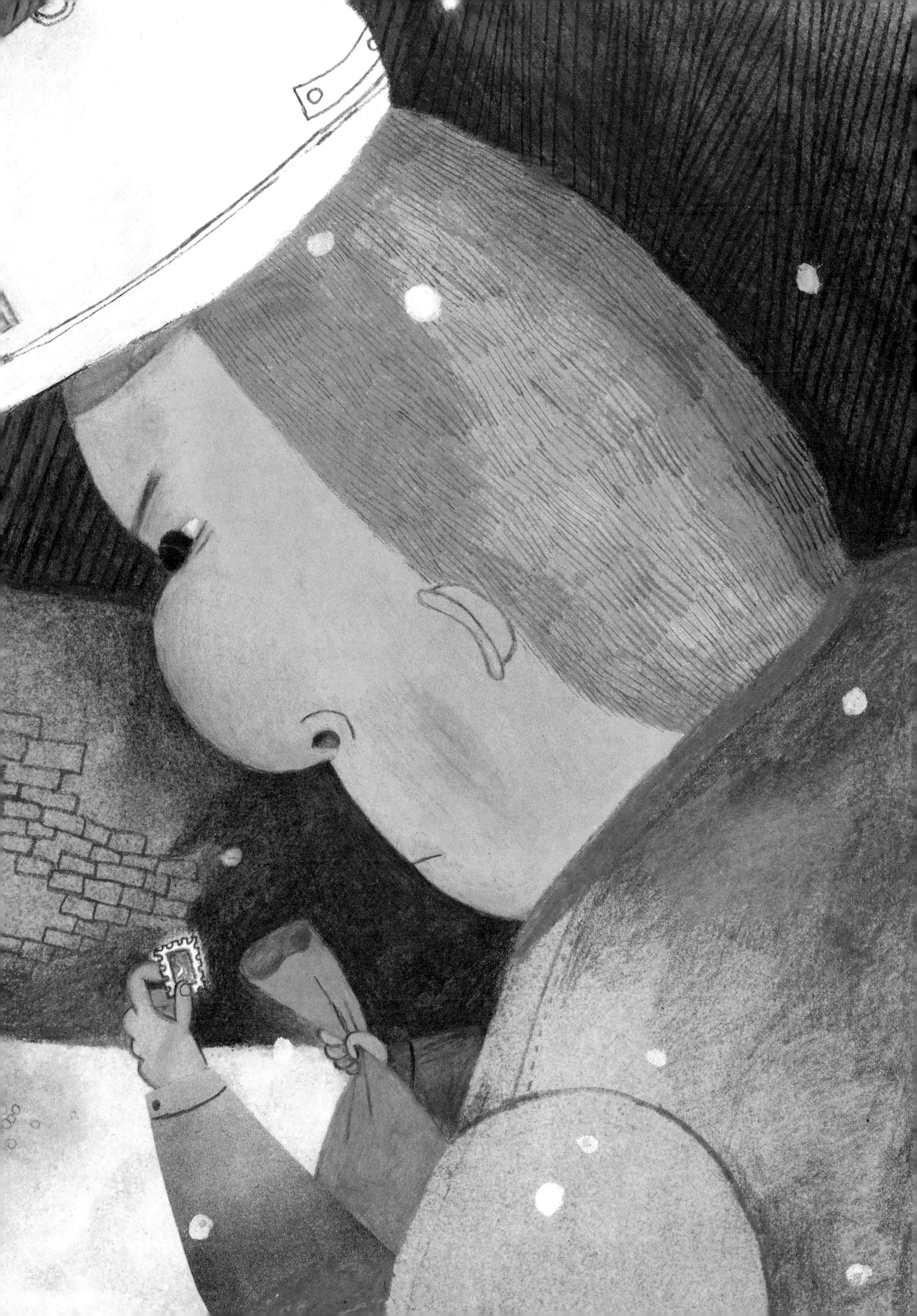

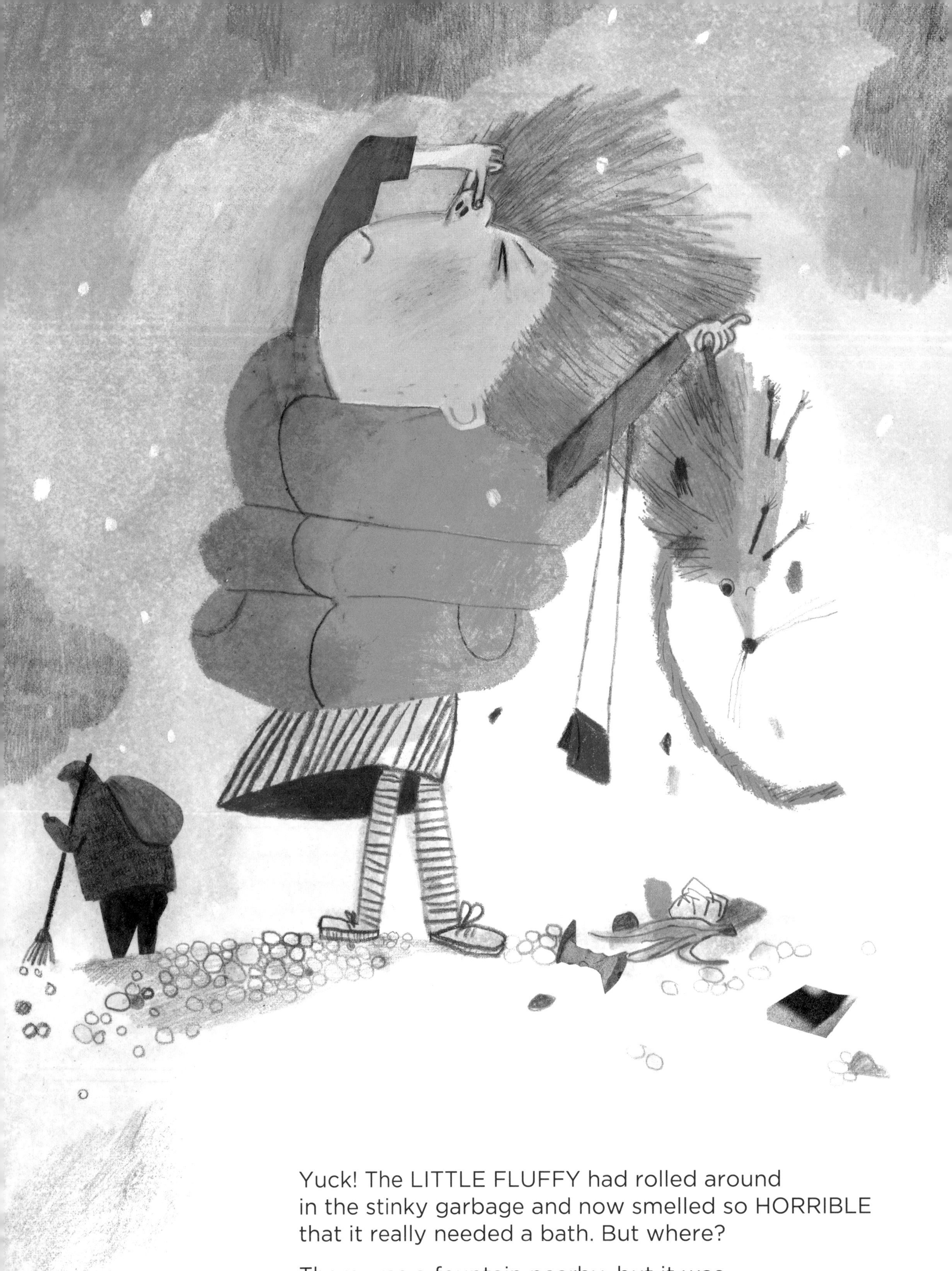

Yuck! The LITTLE FLUFFY had rolled around in the stinky garbage and now smelled so HORRIBLE that it really needed a bath. But where?

There was a fountain nearby, but it was coin operated...

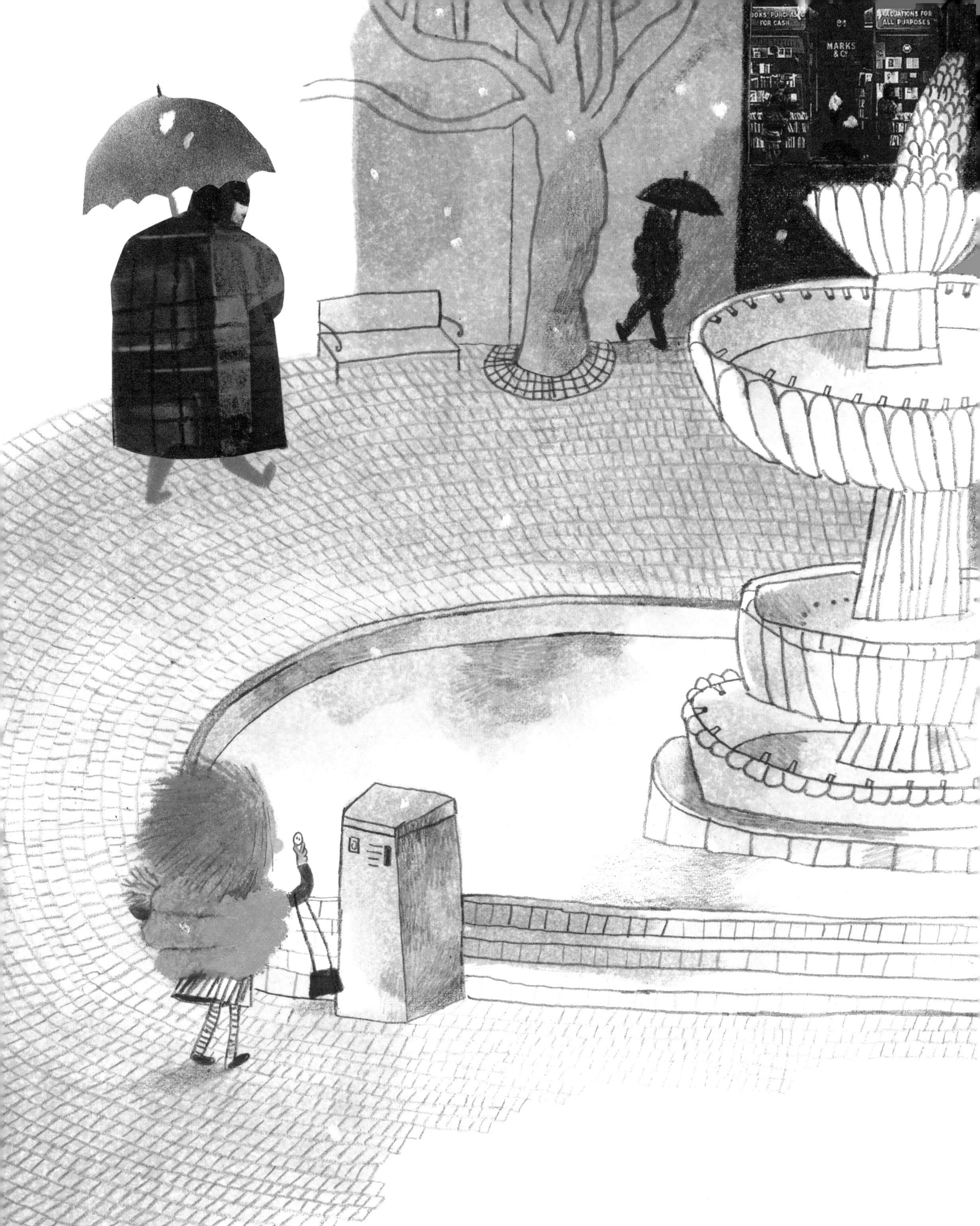
FOR CASH
MARKS & Co
ALL PURPOSES

...and I didn't have a cent in my pockets,
only Mimi's old button. Still, it was worth a try.
After all, it was a very precious button.

I put it into the slot and waited.

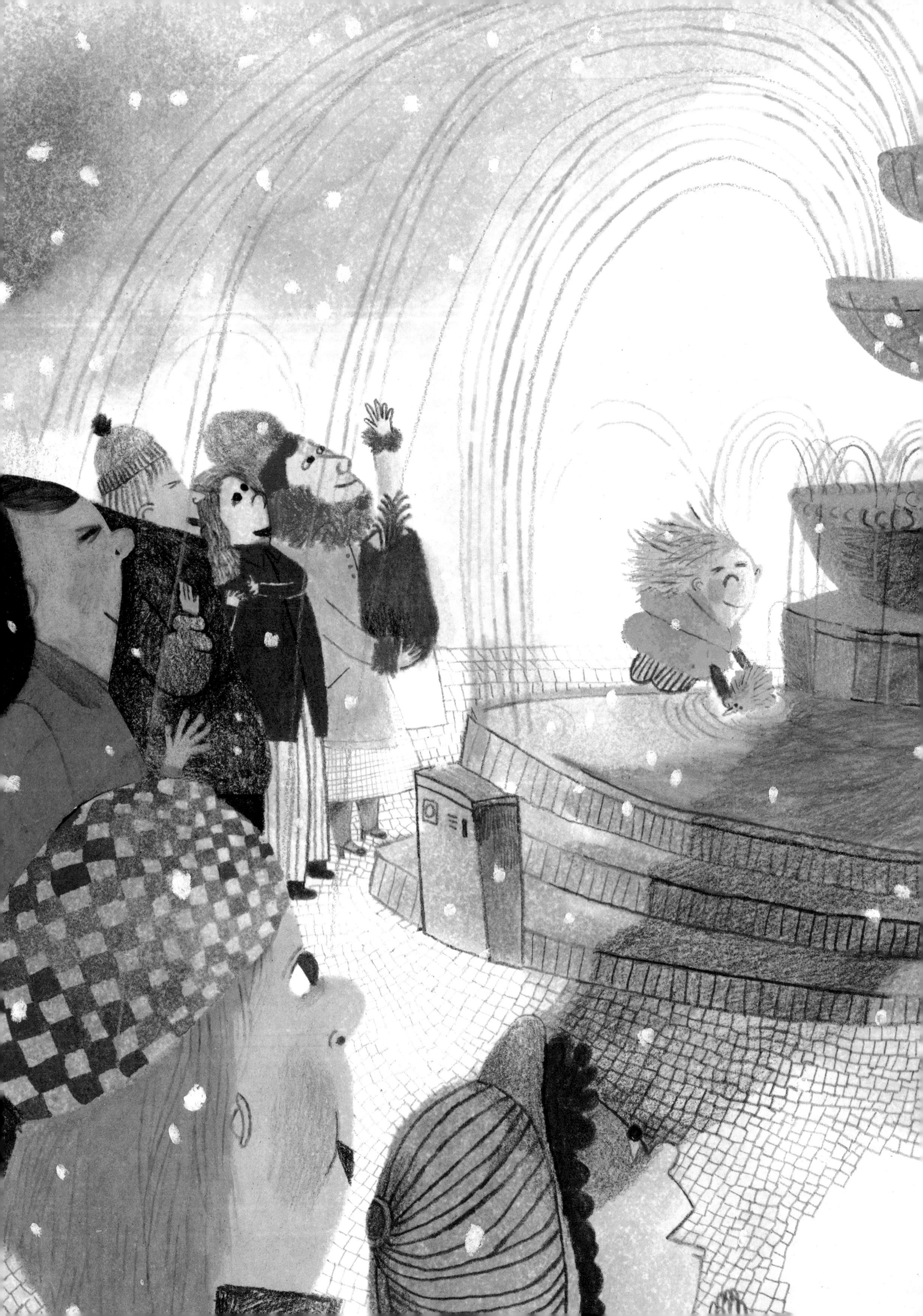

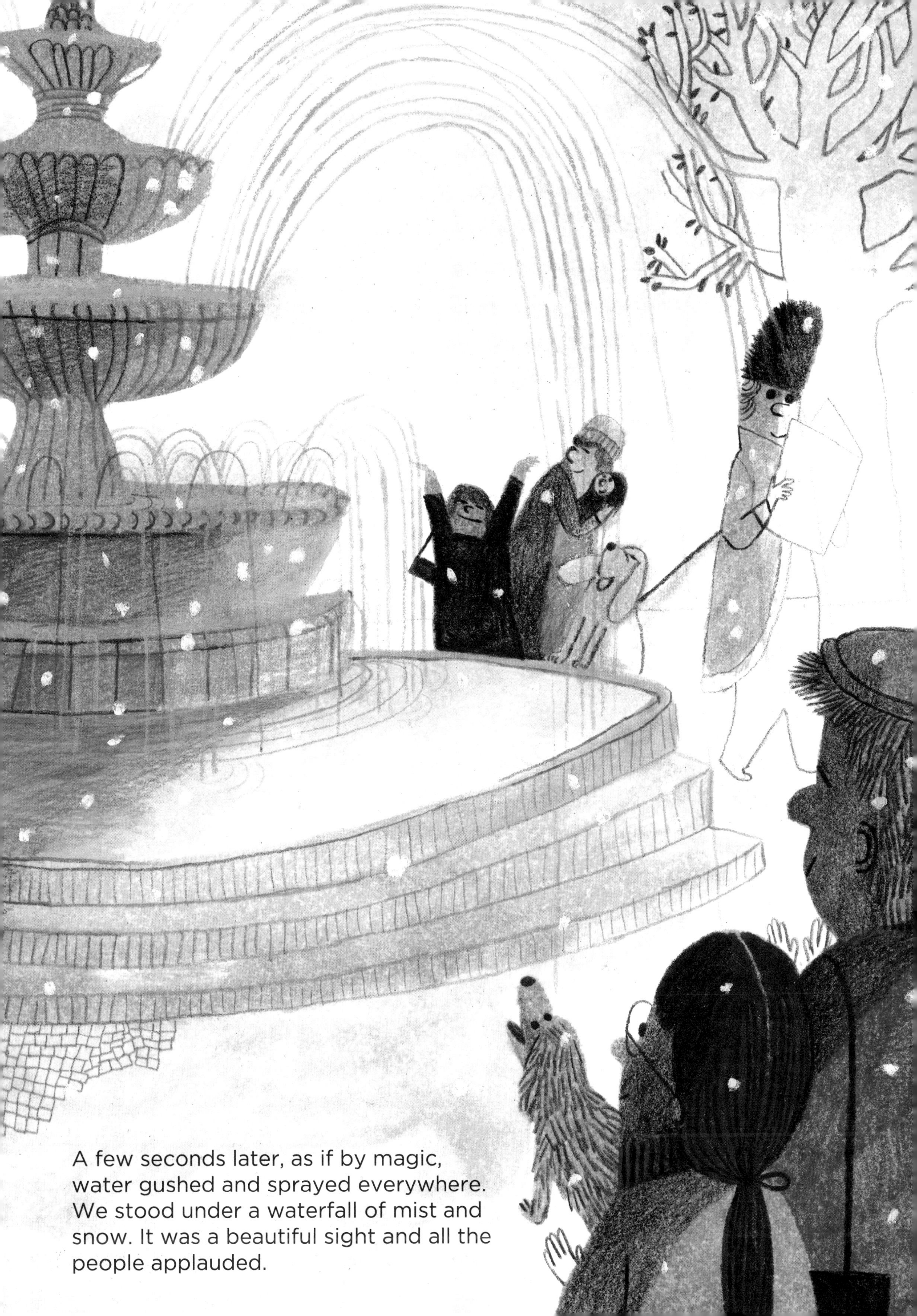

A few seconds later, as if by magic, water gushed and sprayed everywhere. We stood under a waterfall of mist and snow. It was a beautiful sight and all the people applauded.

It was the best day ever!
Because nobody before me
had ever discovered such a wonder,
which meant that I now knew how to do
something better than anyone else:
how to find FLUFFY LITTLE SQUISHIES.

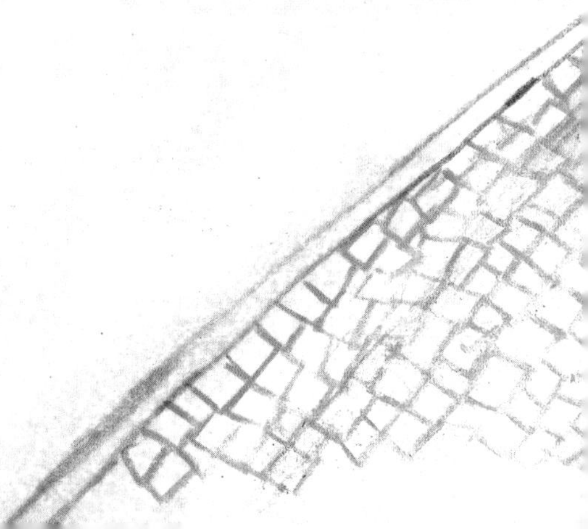

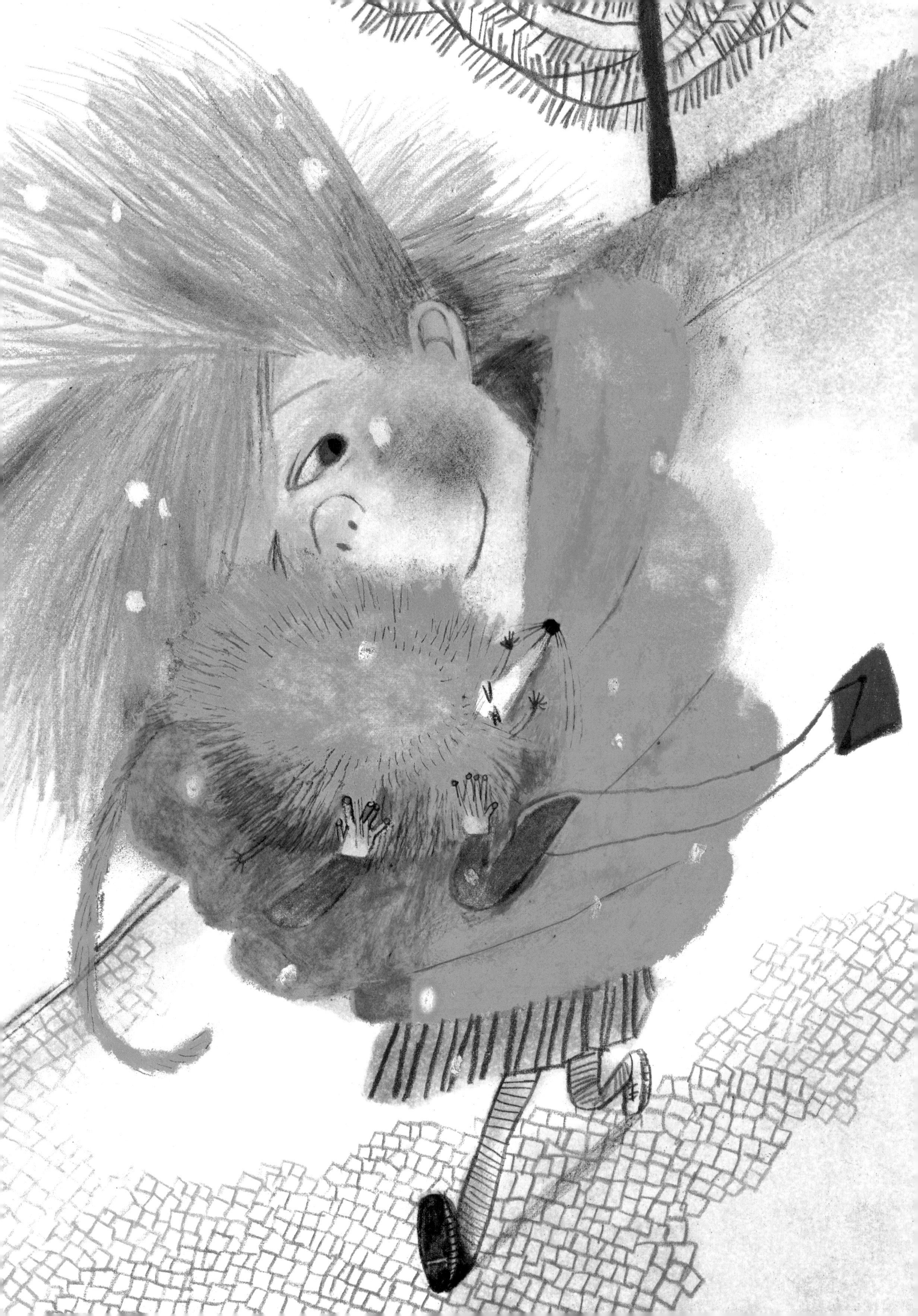

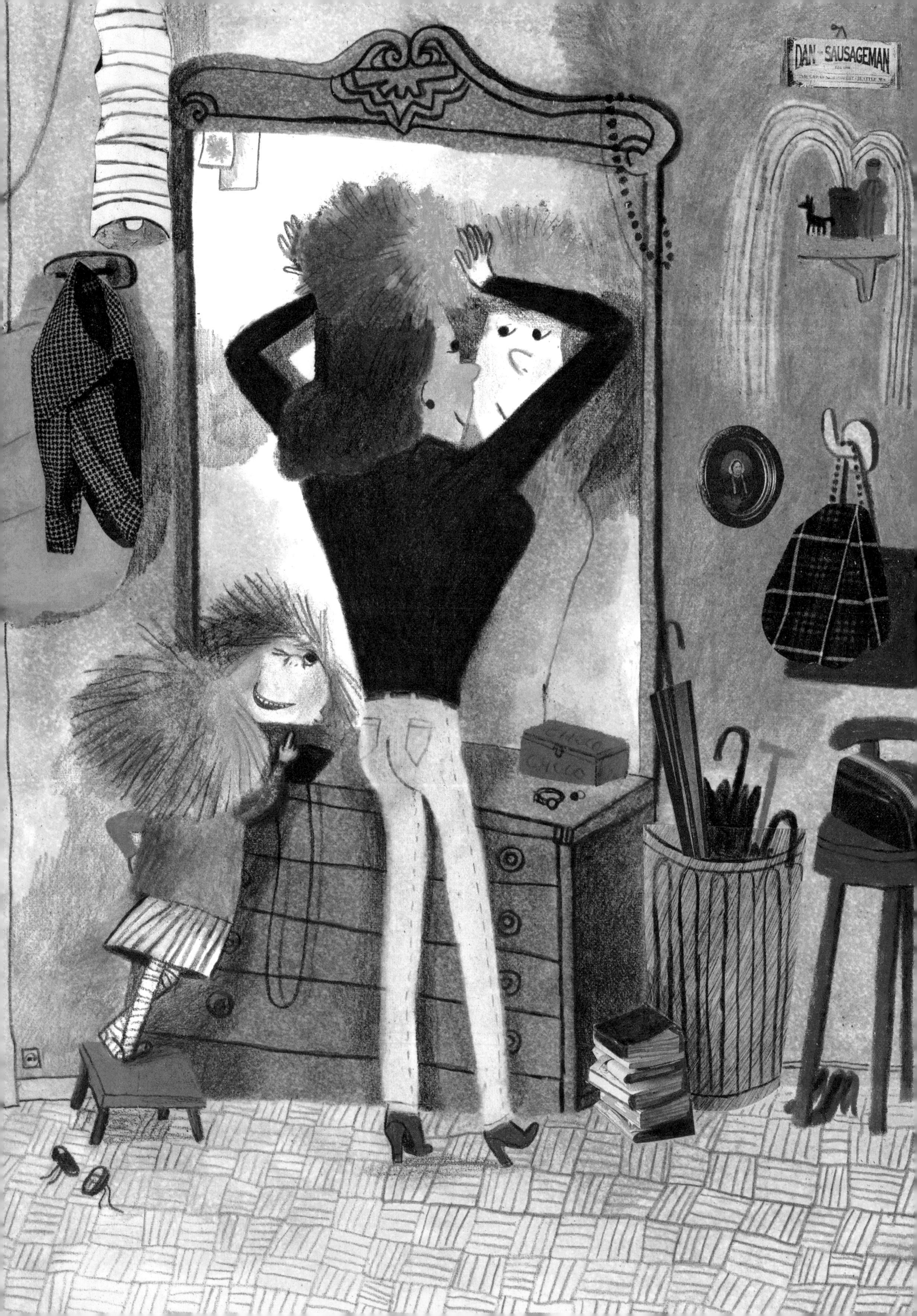
DAN SAUSAGEMAN

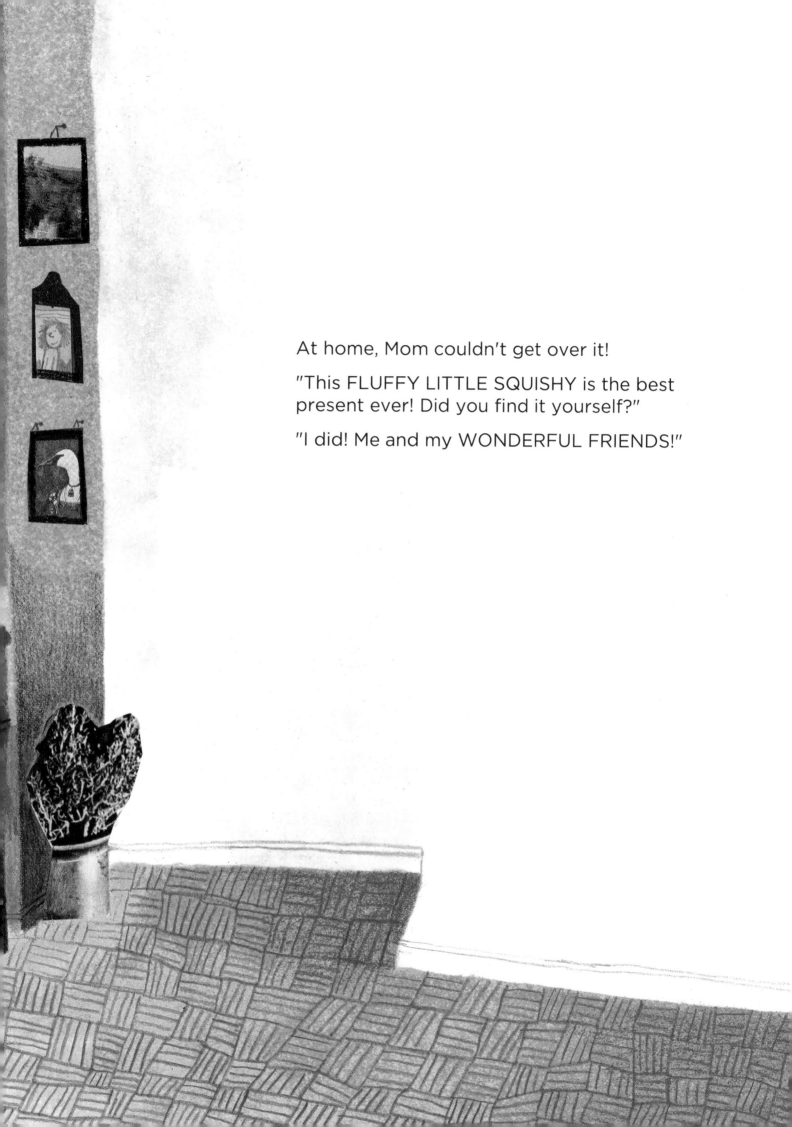

At home, Mom couldn't get over it!

"This FLUFFY LITTLE SQUISHY is the best present ever! Did you find it yourself?"

"I did! Me and my WONDERFUL FRIENDS!"

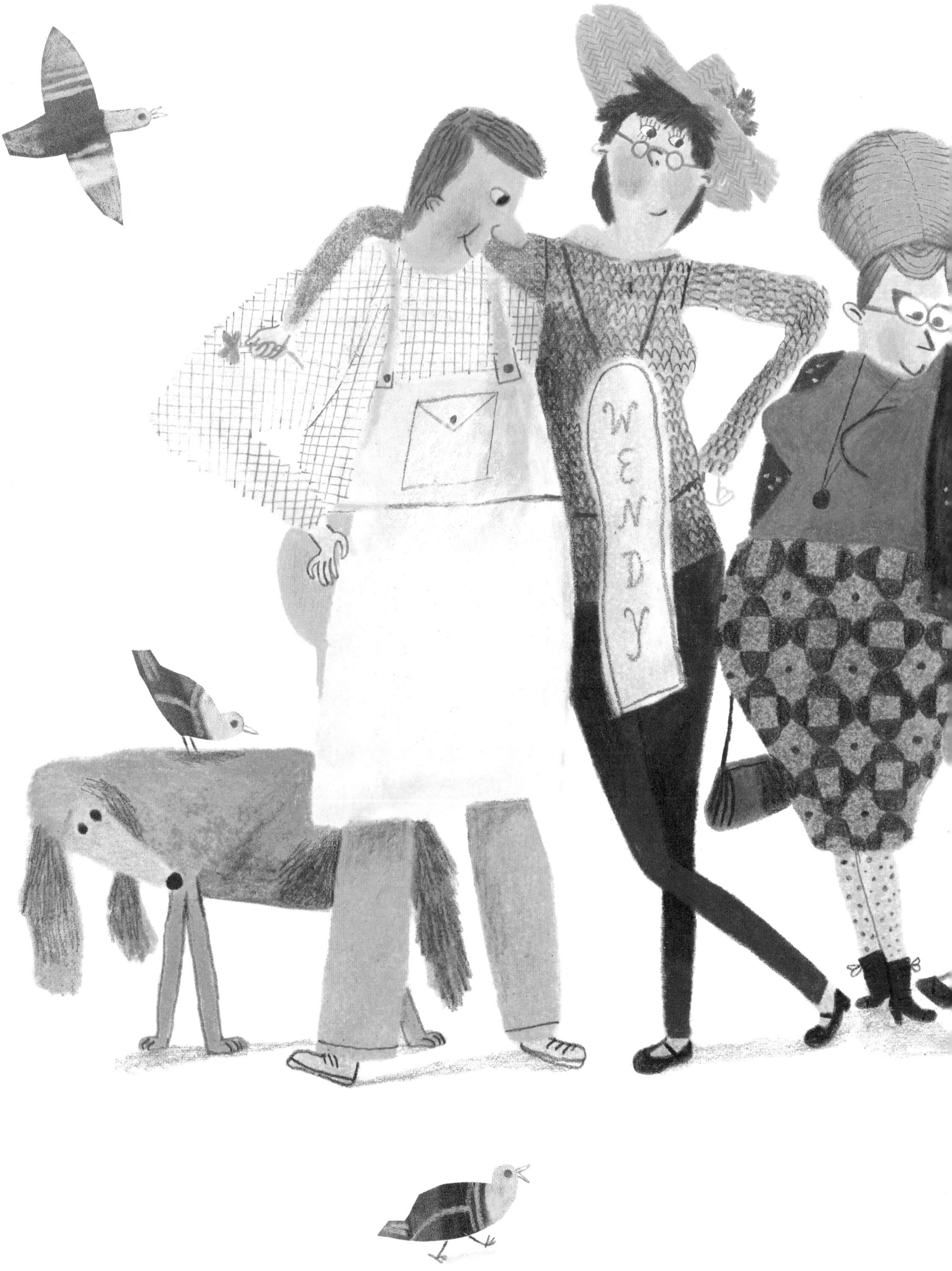
WENDY